Hi, parents!

Your child's love of reading starts here, with HarperAlley's **I Can Read Comics**!

I Can Read Comics introduces children to the world of graphic novel storytelling and encourages visual literacy in emerging readers. Comics inspire reader engagement unlike any other format. They ask readers to infer and answer questions, like:

1. What do I read first? Image or text?
2. Why is this word balloon shaped this way, and that word balloon shaped that way?
3. Why is a character making that facial expression? Are they happy, angry, excited, sad?

From the comics your child reads with you to the first comic they read on their own, there are **I Can Read Comics** for every stage of reading:

LEVEL **1**

Simple stories for shared reading.

LEVEL **2**

Engaging stories for children reading on their own.

LEVEL **3**

Complex stories for independent readers.

The magic of graphic novel storytelling lies between the gutters. Unlock the magic with...

I Can Read Comics!

Visit **ICanRead.com** for information on enriching your child's reading experience.

I Can Read *Comics* Cartooning Basics

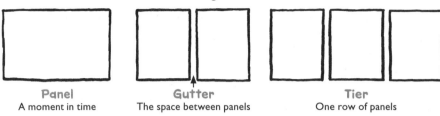

Panel
A moment in time

Gutter
The space between panels

Tier
One row of panels

Word Balloons
When someone talks, thinks, whispers, or screams, their words go in here:

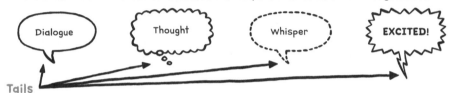

Dialogue

Thought

Whisper

EXCITED!

Tails
Point to whoever is talking / thinking / whispering / screaming / etc.

A quick how-to-read comics guide:

In a **panel**, read the text on the **left** first.

Then, read the text on the **right**.

Remember to...
Read the text along with the image, paying close attention to the character's acting, the action, and/or the scene. Every little detail matters!

No dialogue? No problem!
If there is no dialogue within a panel, take the time to read the image. Visual cues are just as important as text, so don't forget about them!

On a page, **start here**, in the **top left** corner!

After that, read the panel immediately to the **right**.

When you're done up there, come down here and read **this** panel **next**!

ME NEXT! ME NEXT!

You're almost there...

YOU MADE IT! You just read a comic page!

YAY!

HarperAlley is an imprint of HarperCollins Publishers.
I Can Read® and I Can Read Book® are trademarks of HarperCollins Publishers.

My Little Pony: Sister Switch
MY LITTLE PONY TM & © 2023 Hasbro
All rights reserved. Printed in the United States of America.

ISBN 978-0-06-303755-7

Book design by Elaine Lopez-Levine
22 23 24 25 26 LB 10 9 8 7 6 5 4 3 2 1 ❖ First Edition

I Can Read! Comics

LEVEL 1

MY LITTLE PONY

SISTER SWITCH

MEGAN ROTH   AGNES GARBOWSKA

HARPER alley

An Imprint of HarperCollinsPublishers

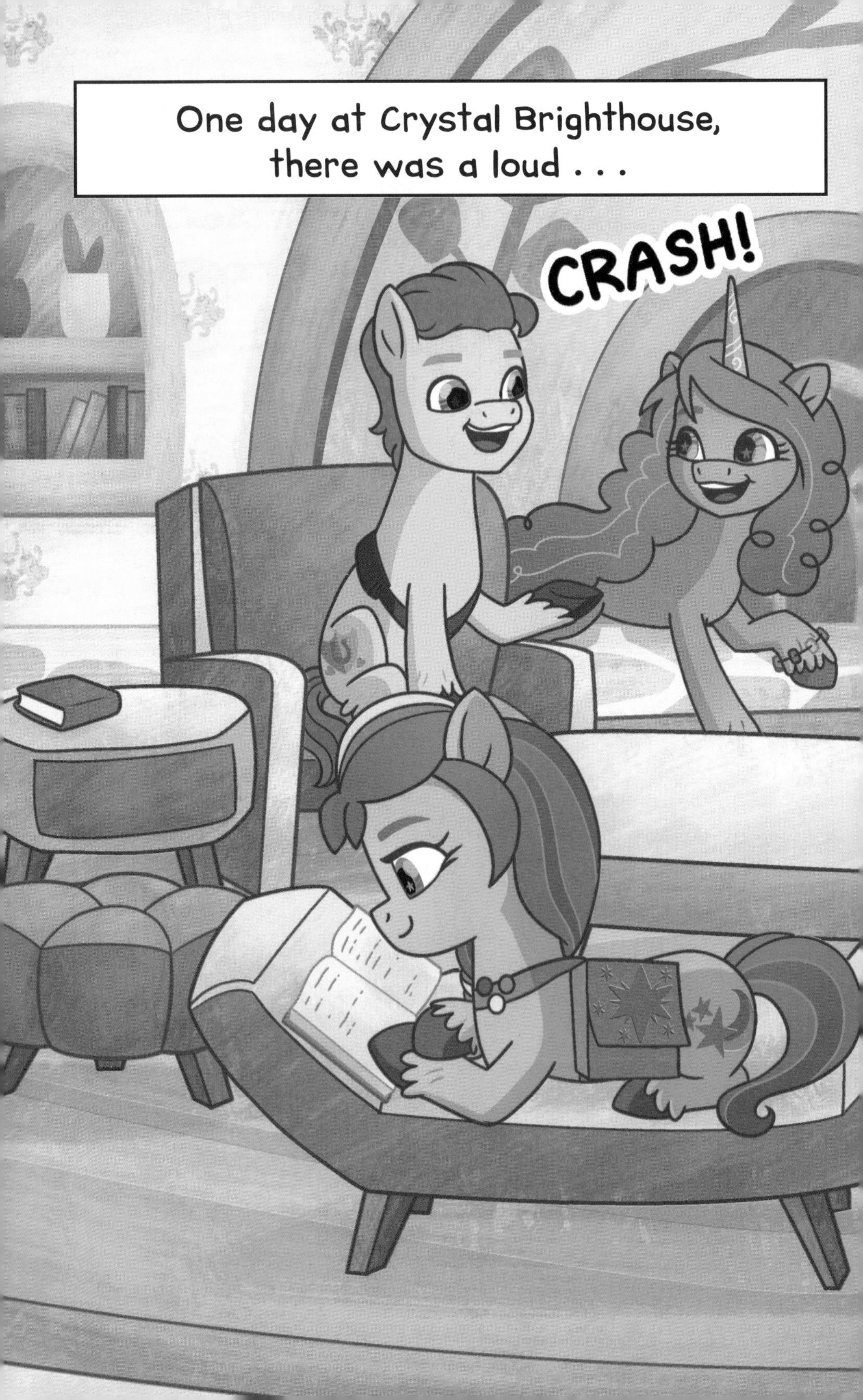
One day at Crystal Brighthouse, there was a loud . . .
CRASH!

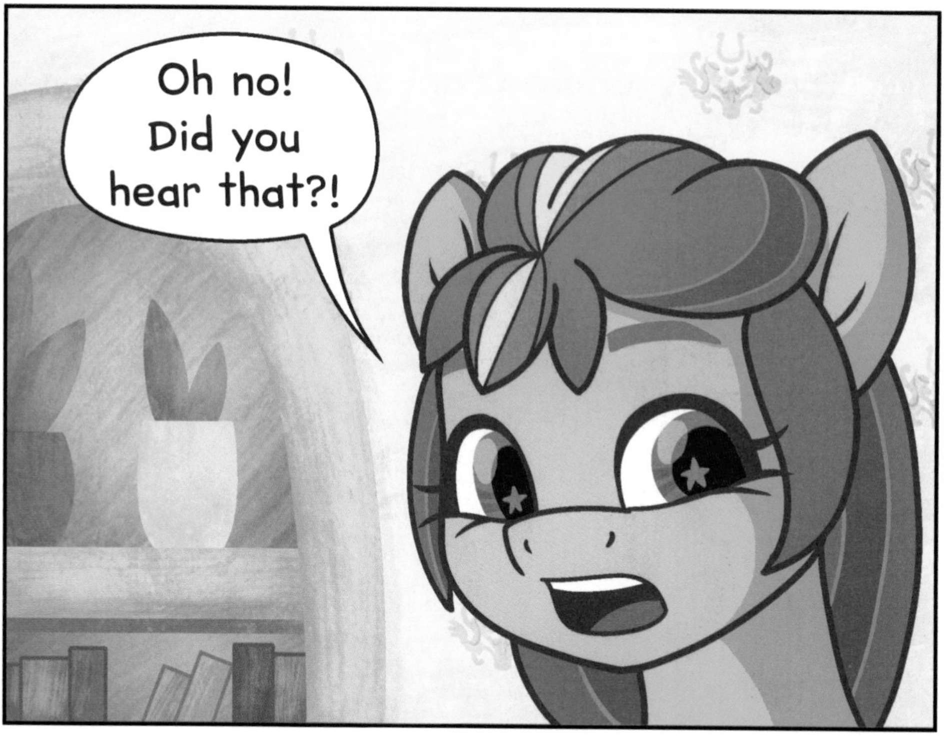
Oh no!
Did you
hear that?!

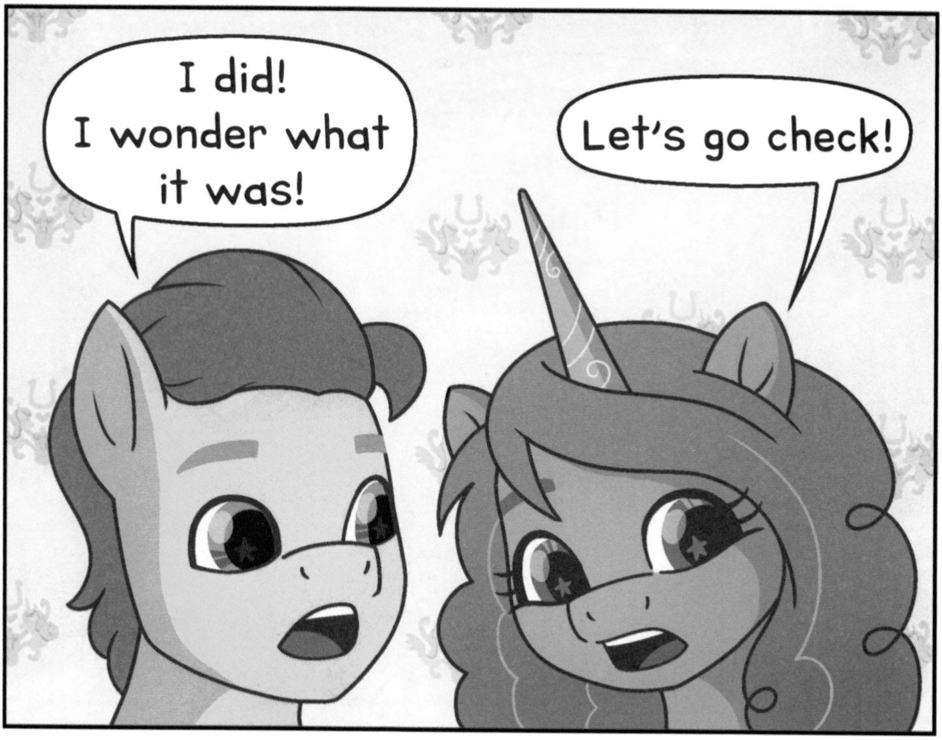
I did!
I wonder what
it was!
Let's go check!

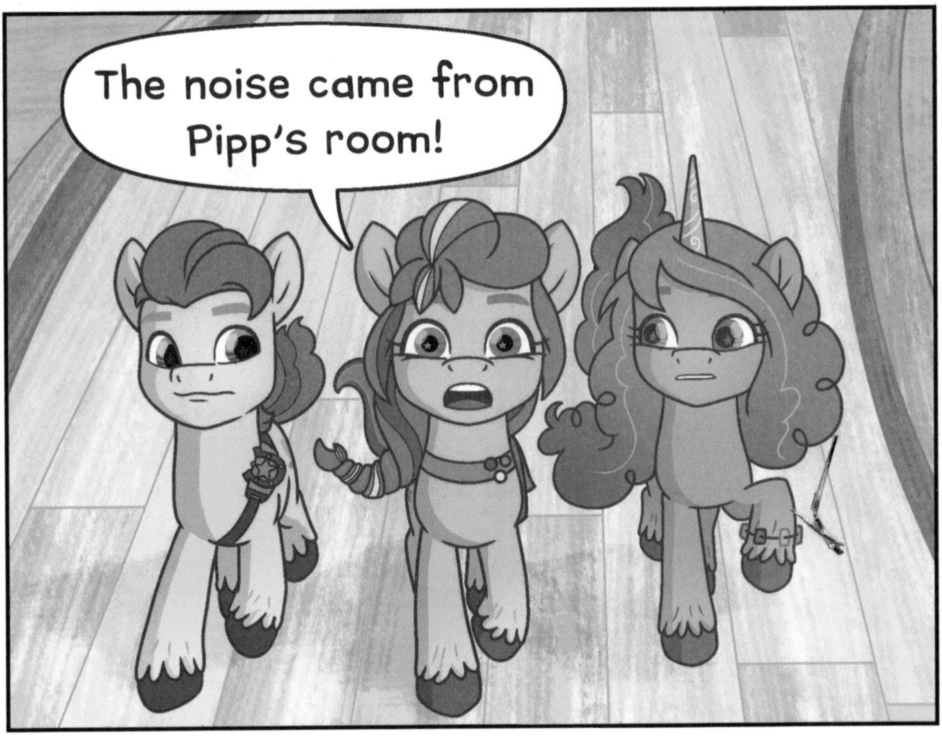
The noise came from Pipp's room!

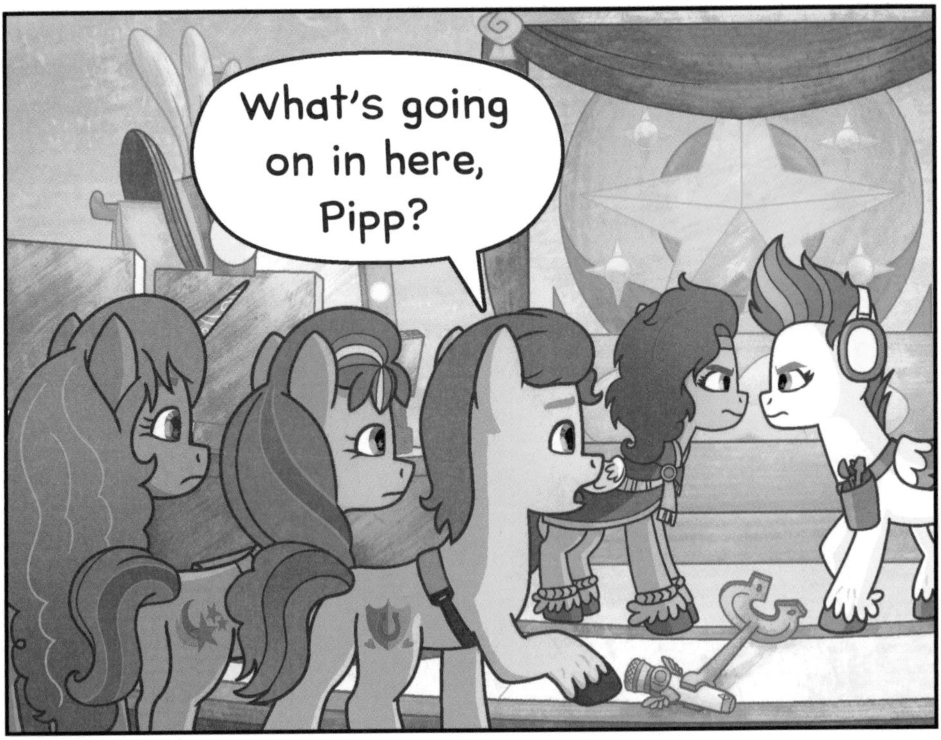
What's going on in here, Pipp?

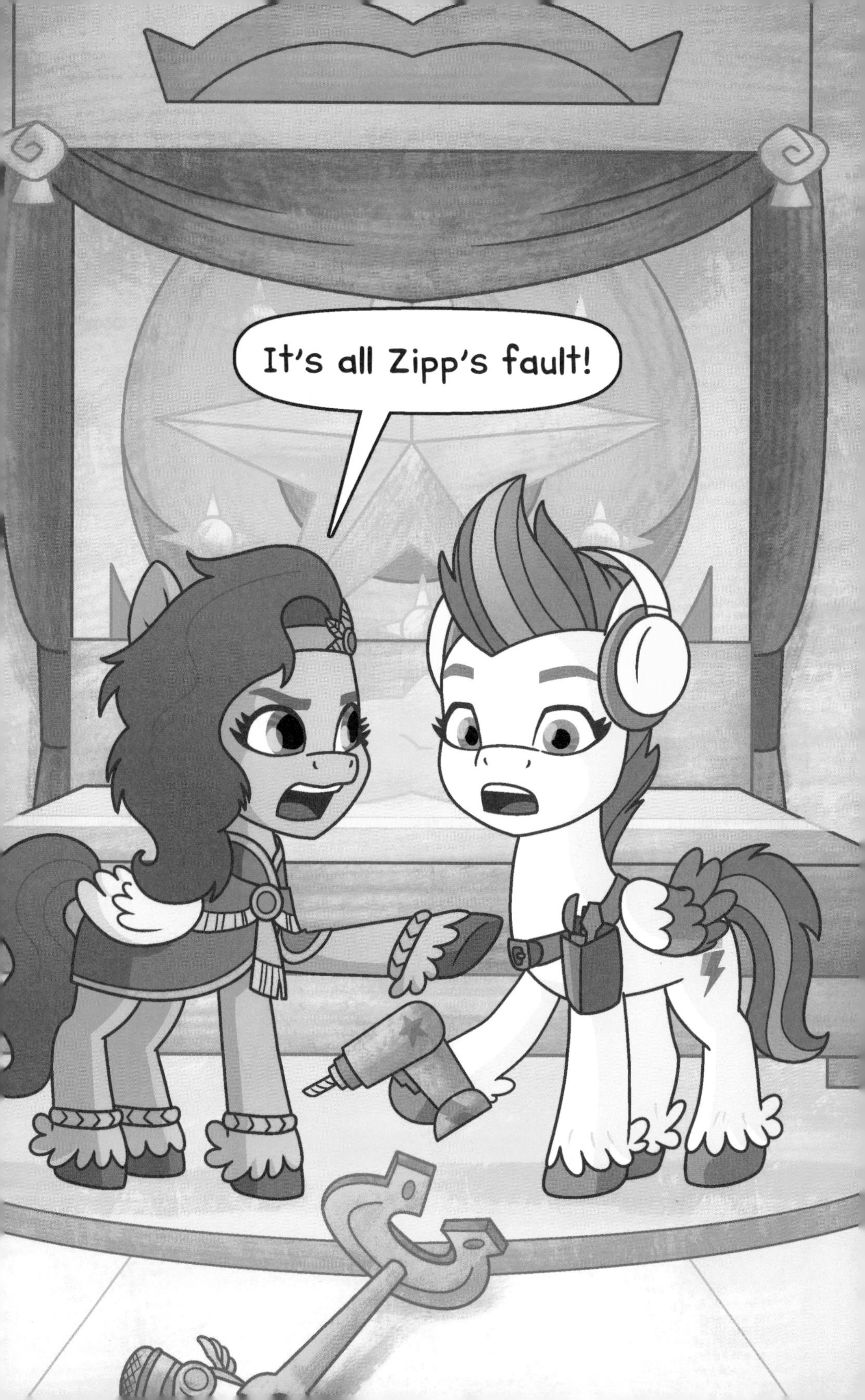
It's all Zipp's fault!

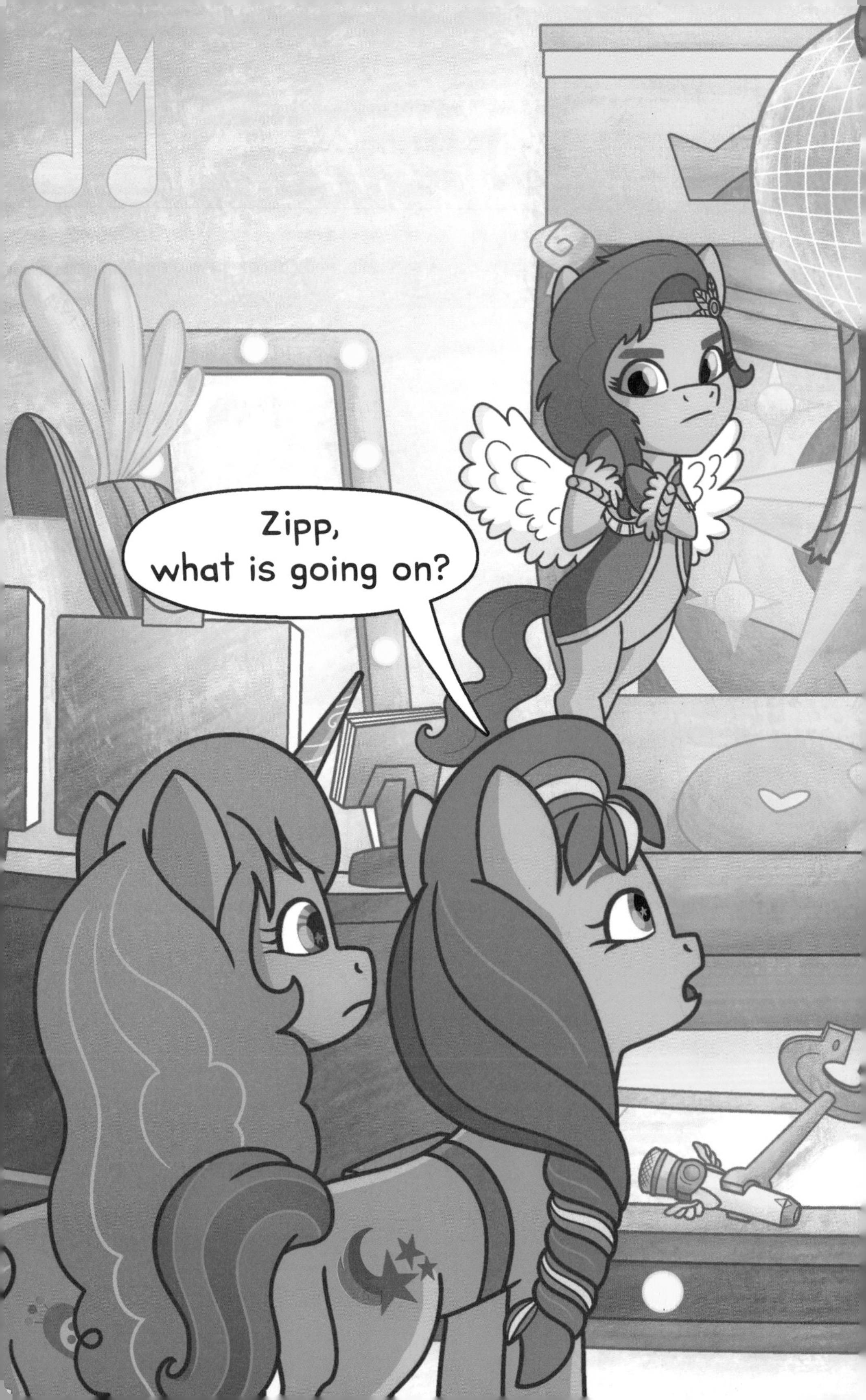
Zipp,
what is going on?

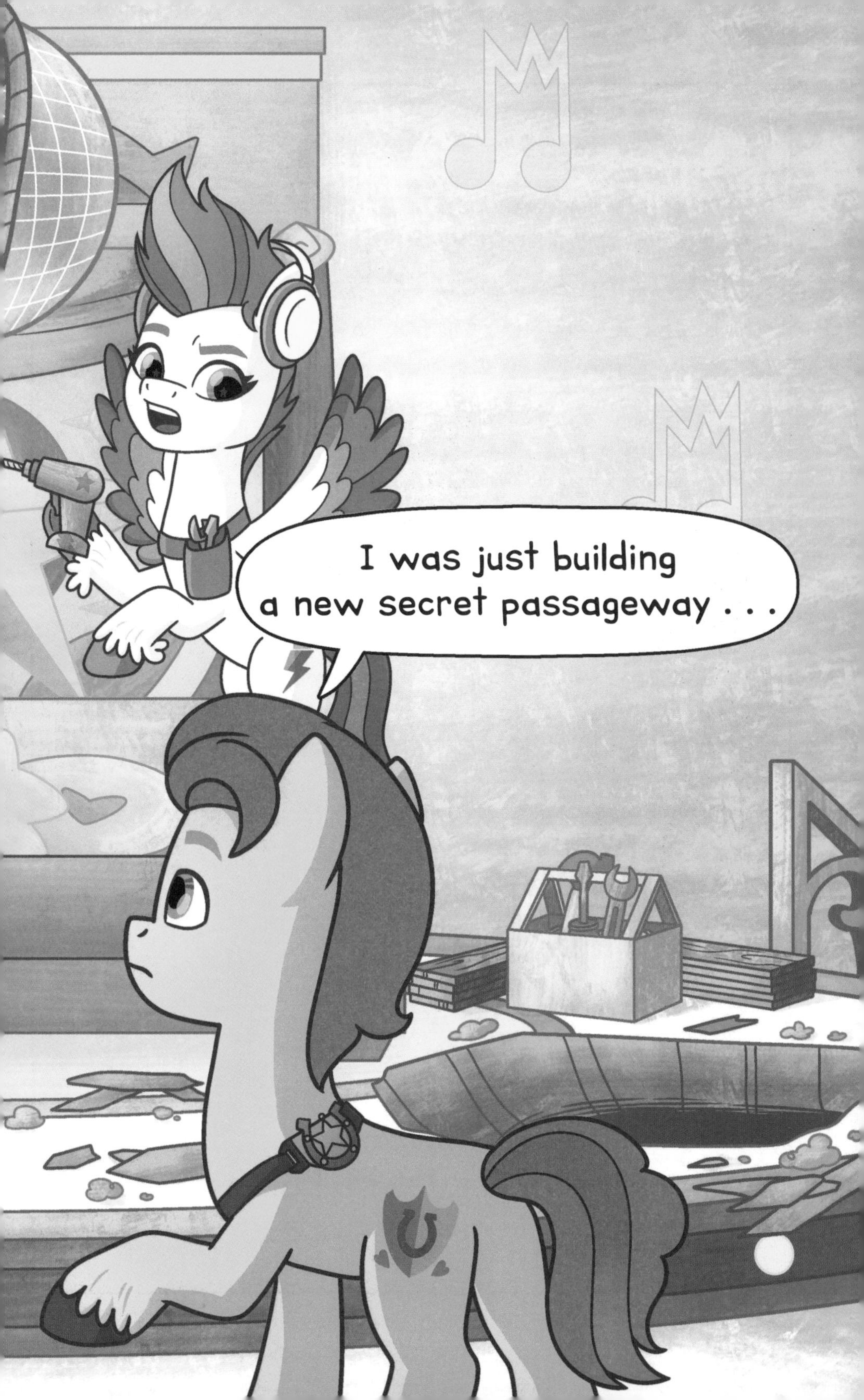
I was just building
a new secret passageway . . .

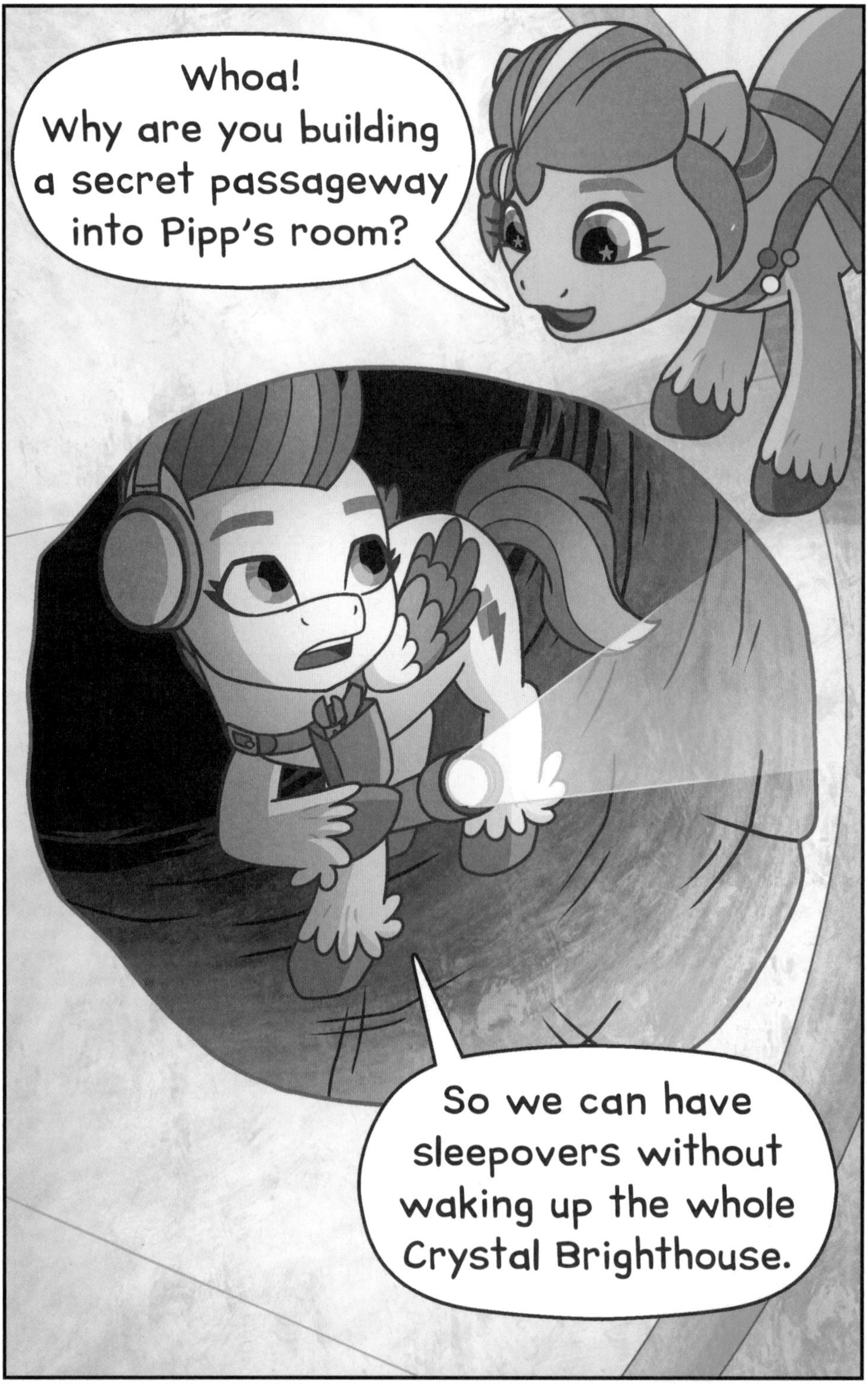
Whoa!
Why are you building a secret passageway into Pipp's room?
So we can have sleepovers without waking up the whole Crystal Brighthouse.

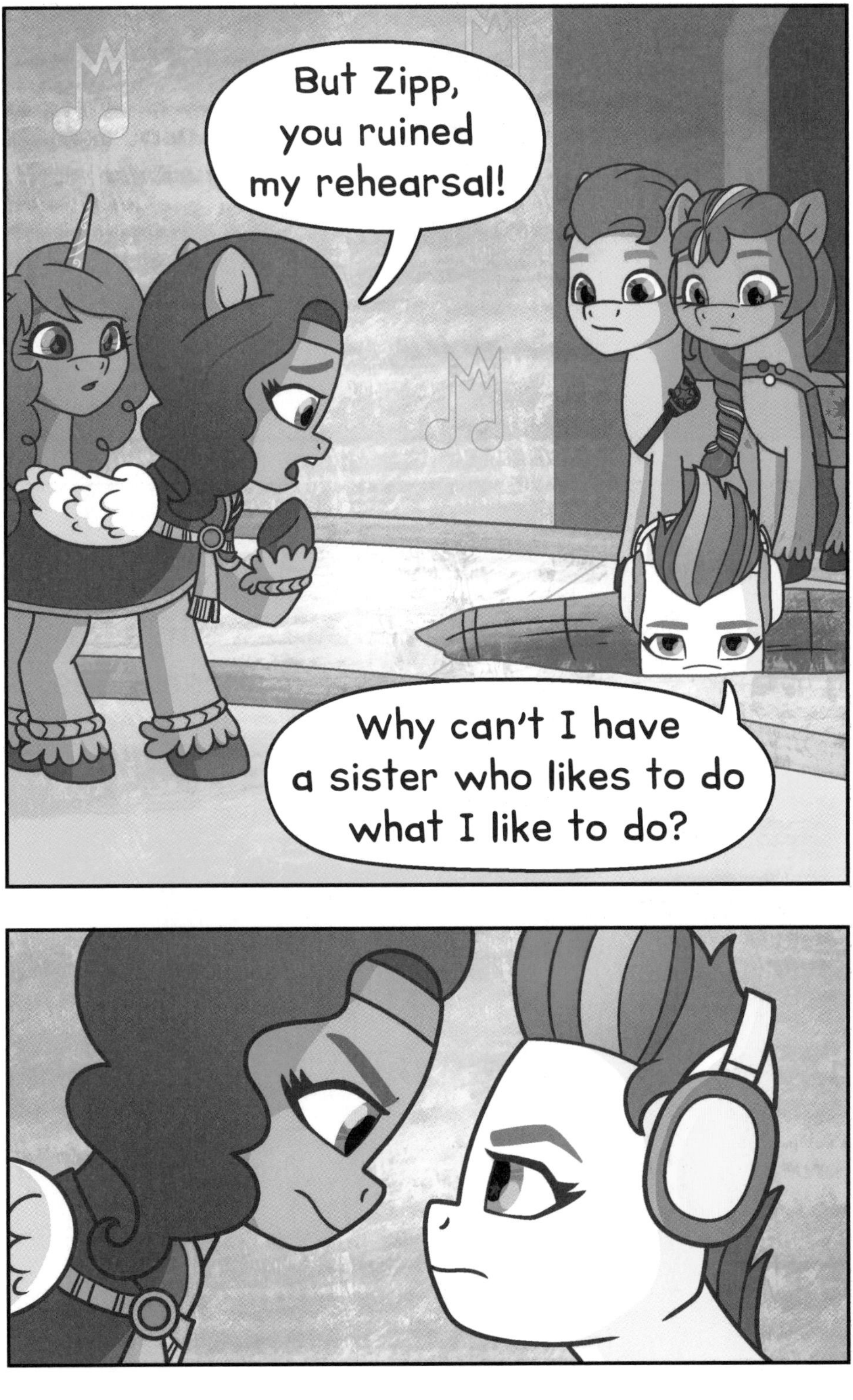
But Zipp, you ruined my rehearsal!
Why can't I have a sister who likes to do what I like to do?

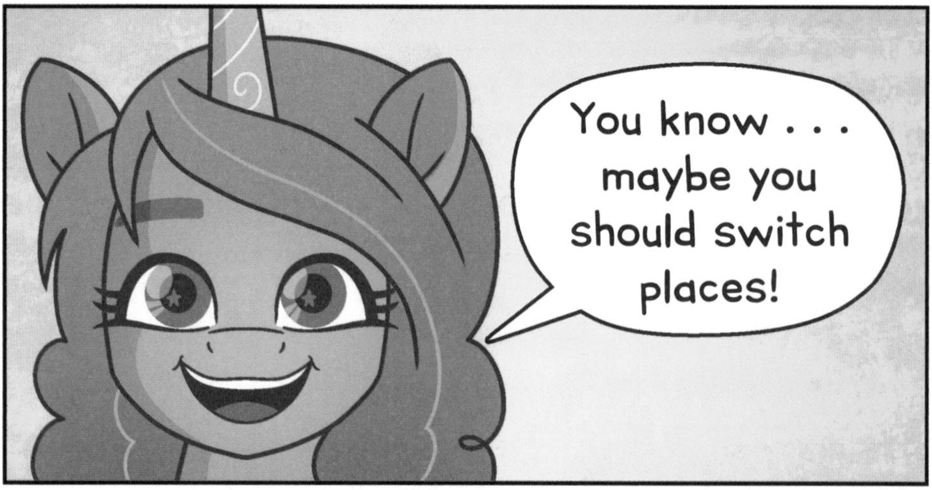
You know . . . maybe you should switch places!

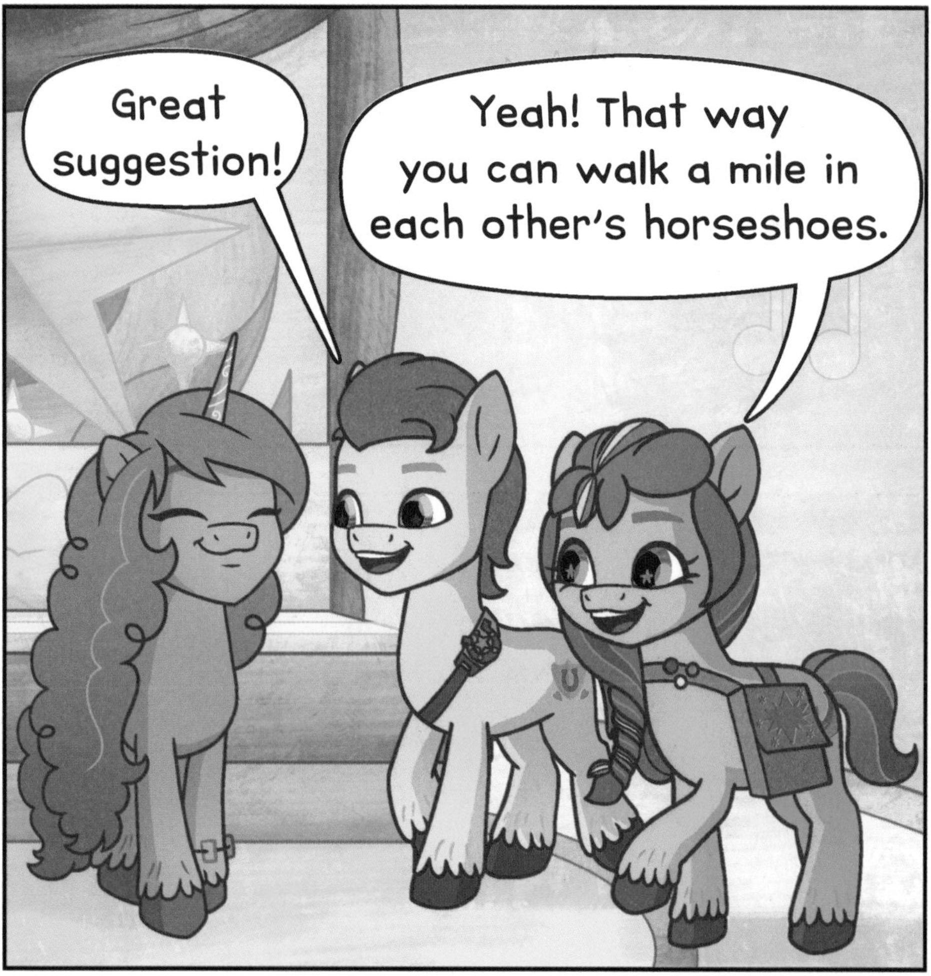
Great suggestion!
Yeah! That way you can walk a mile in each other's horseshoes.

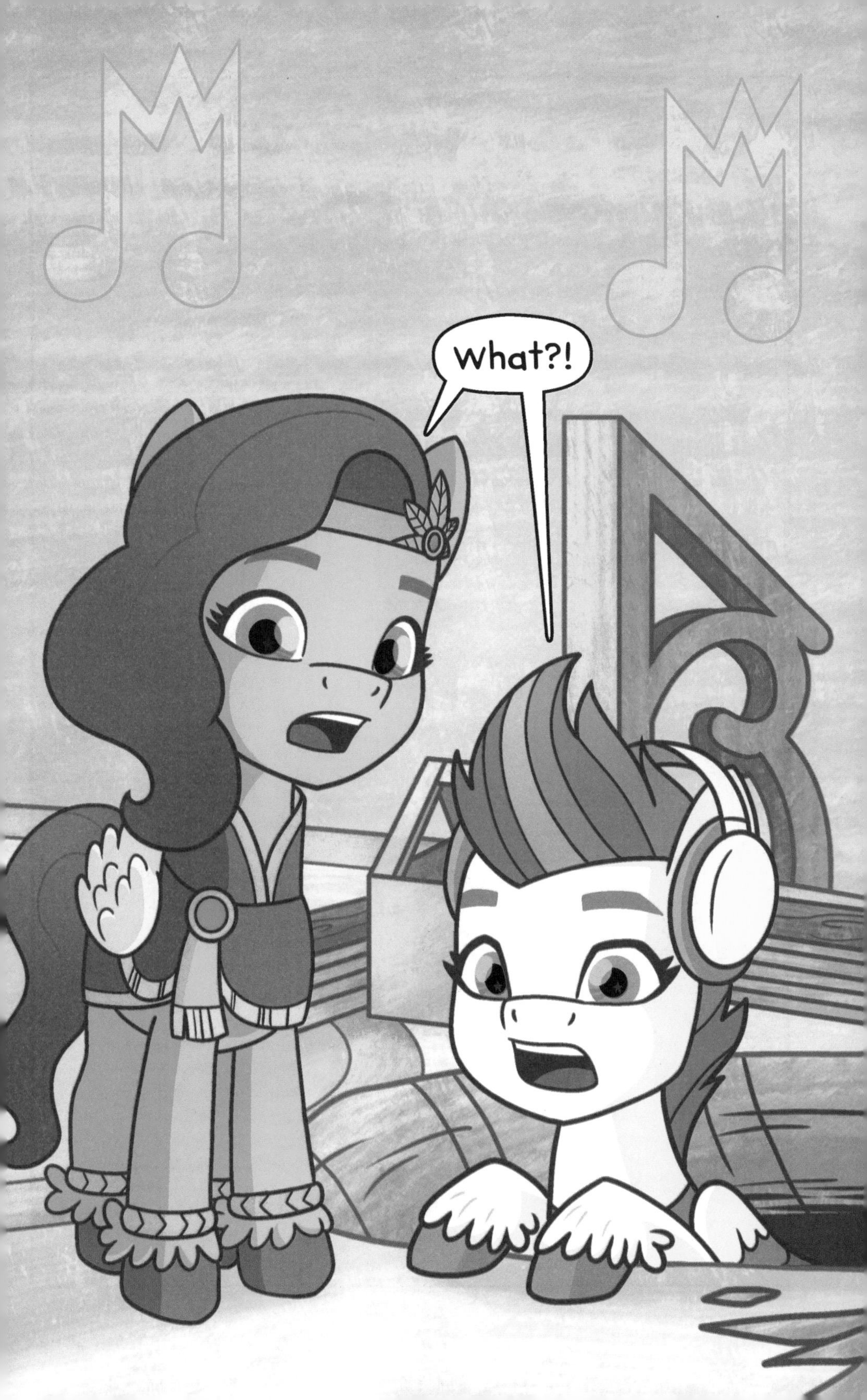
What?!

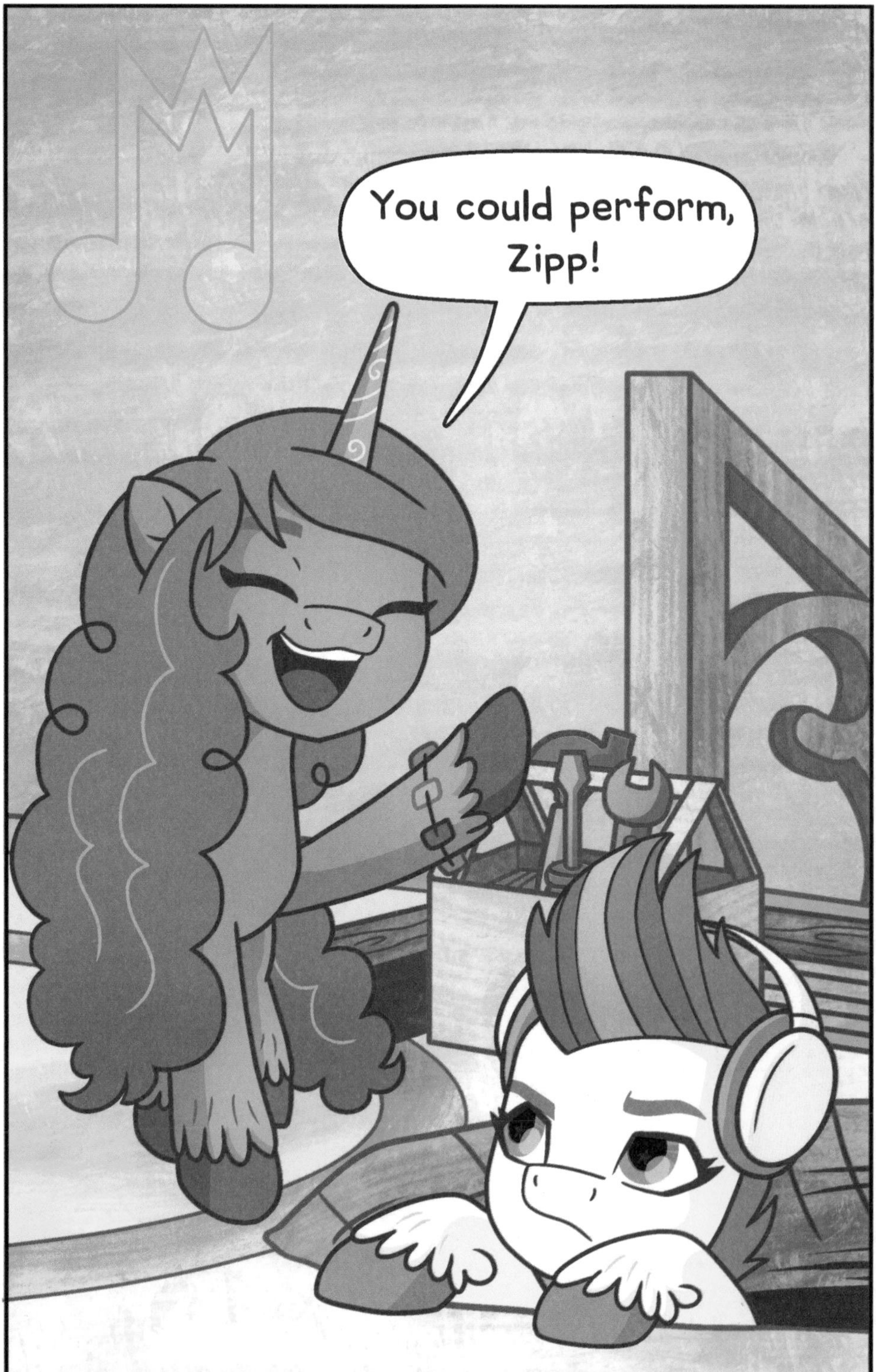
You could perform, Zipp!

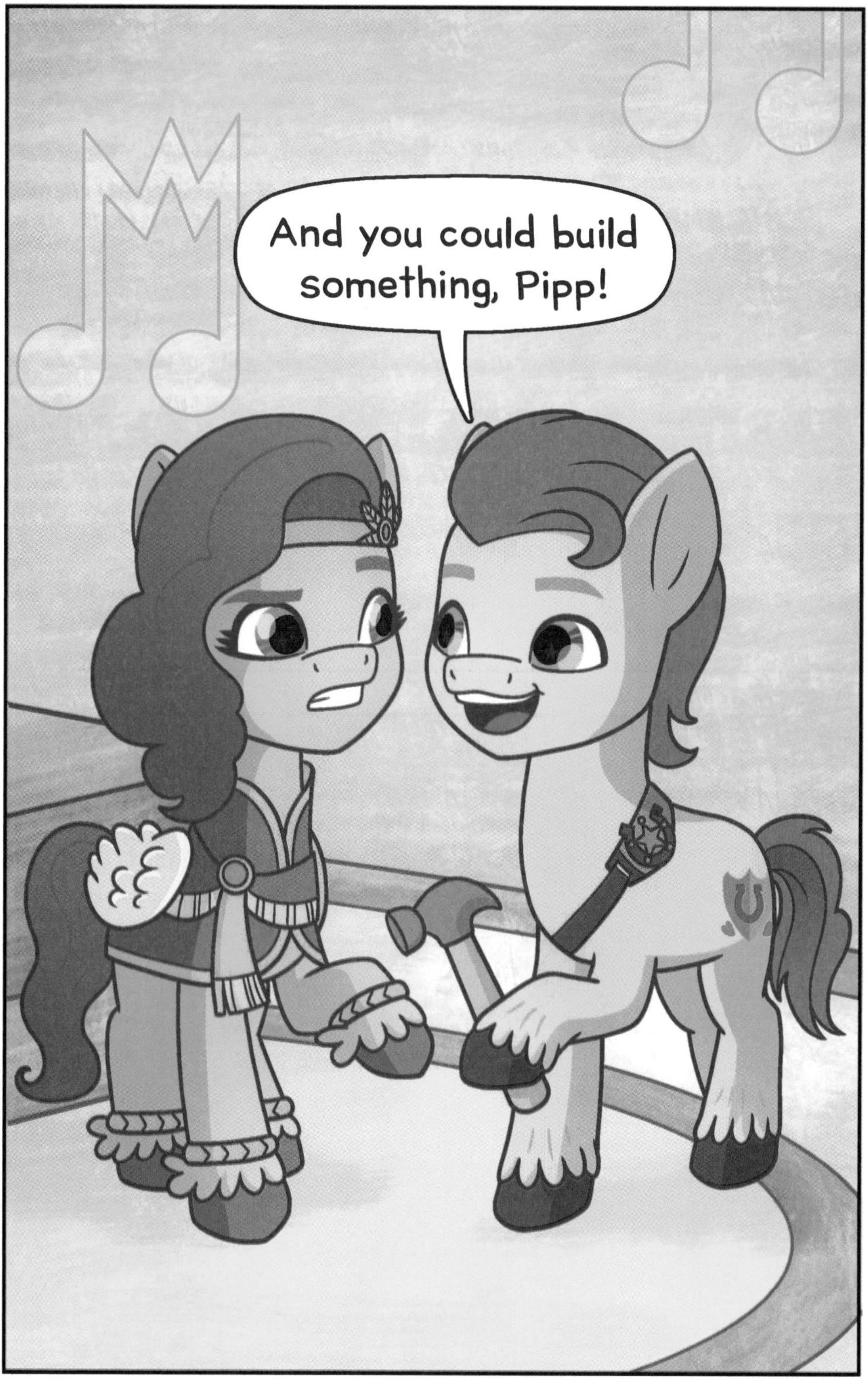
And you could build something, Pipp!

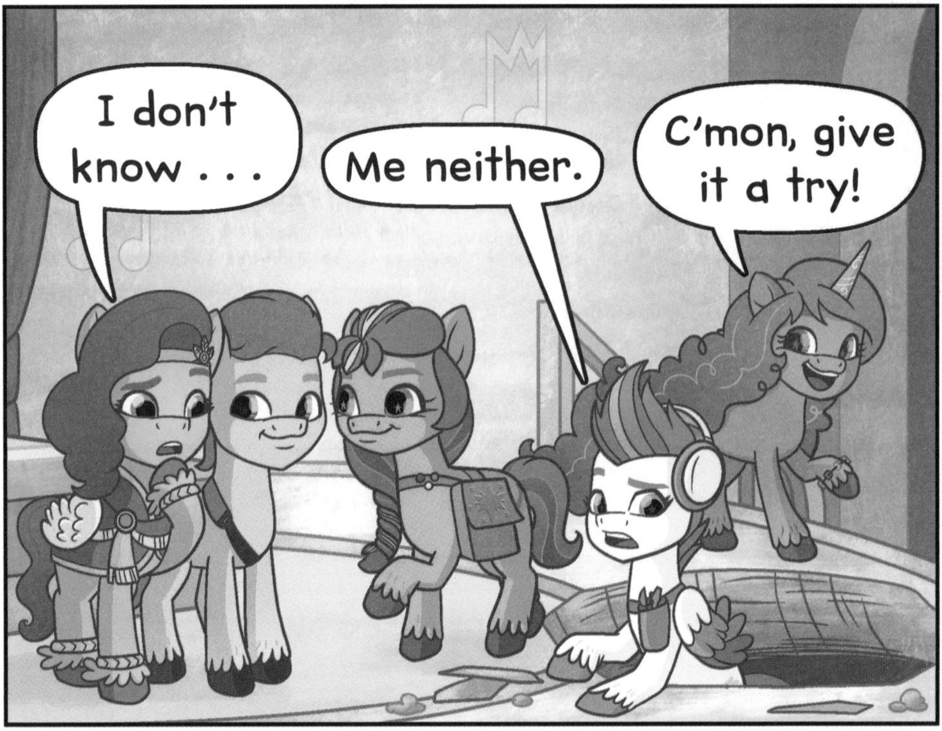
I don't know . . .
Me neither.
C'mon, give it a try!

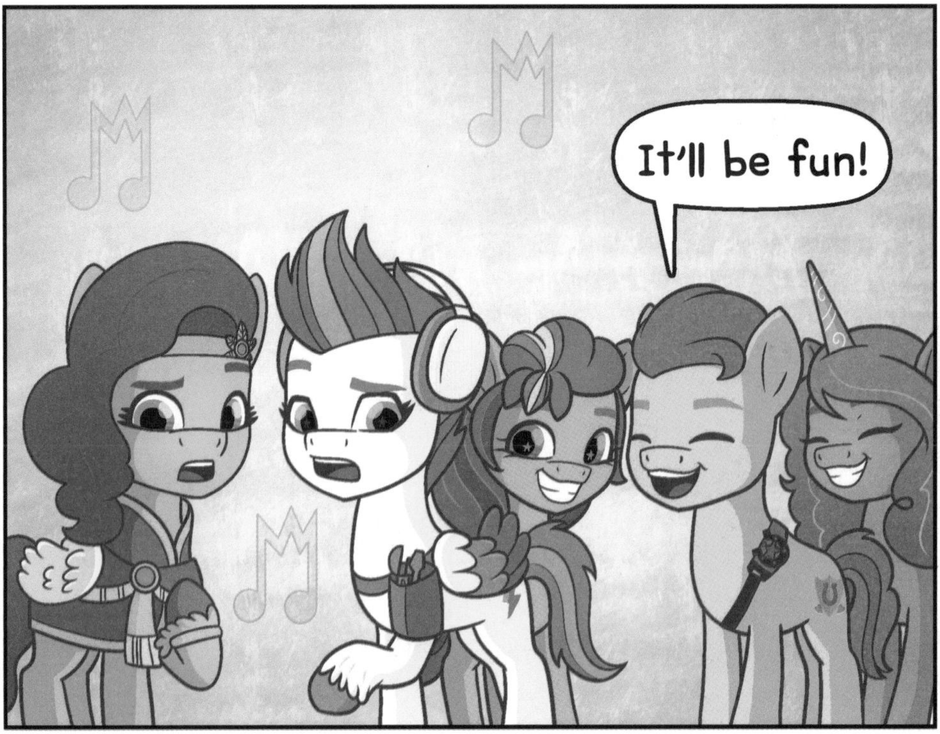
It'll be fun!

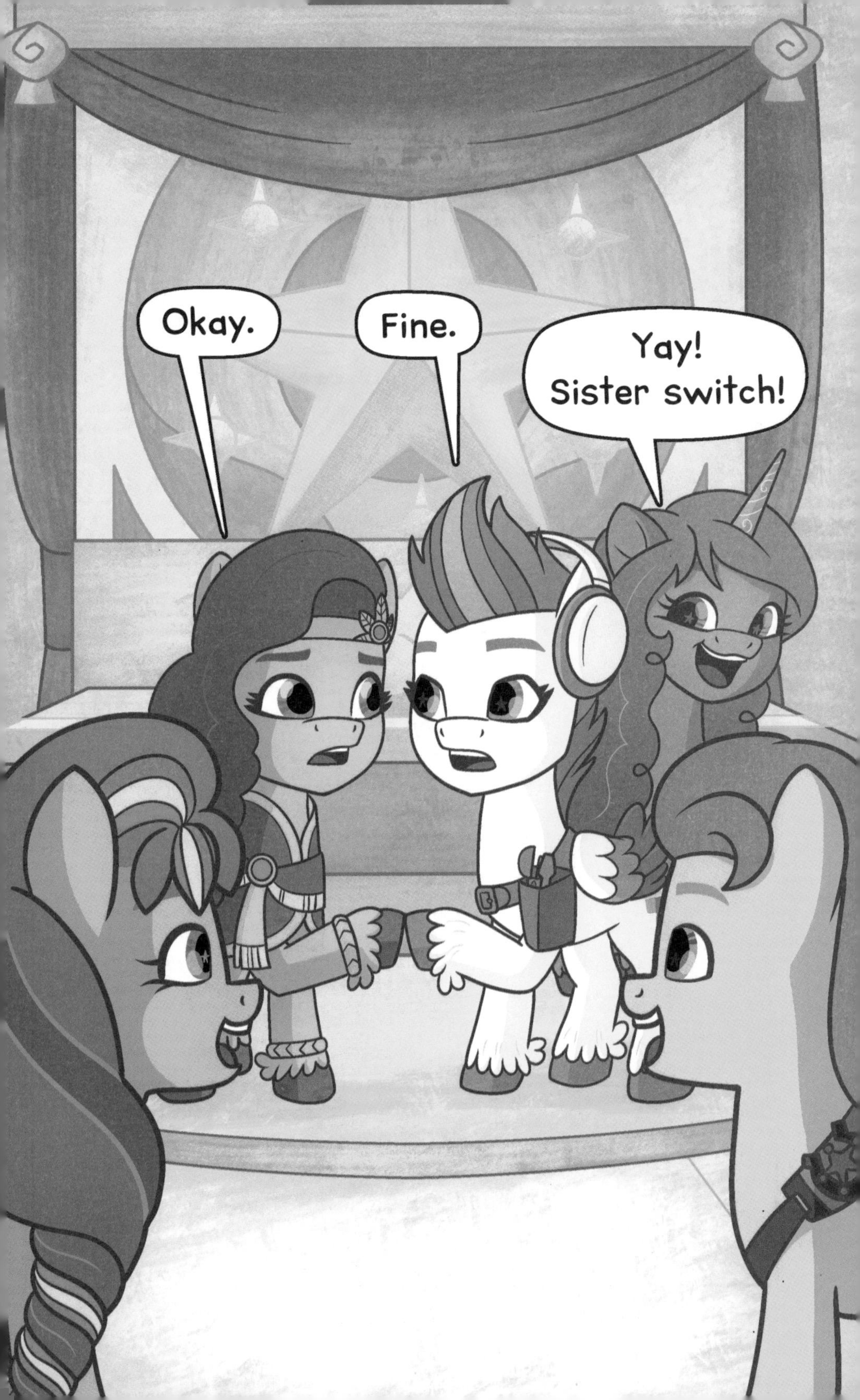
Okay.
Fine.
Yay! Sister switch!

And so Pipp started to build,

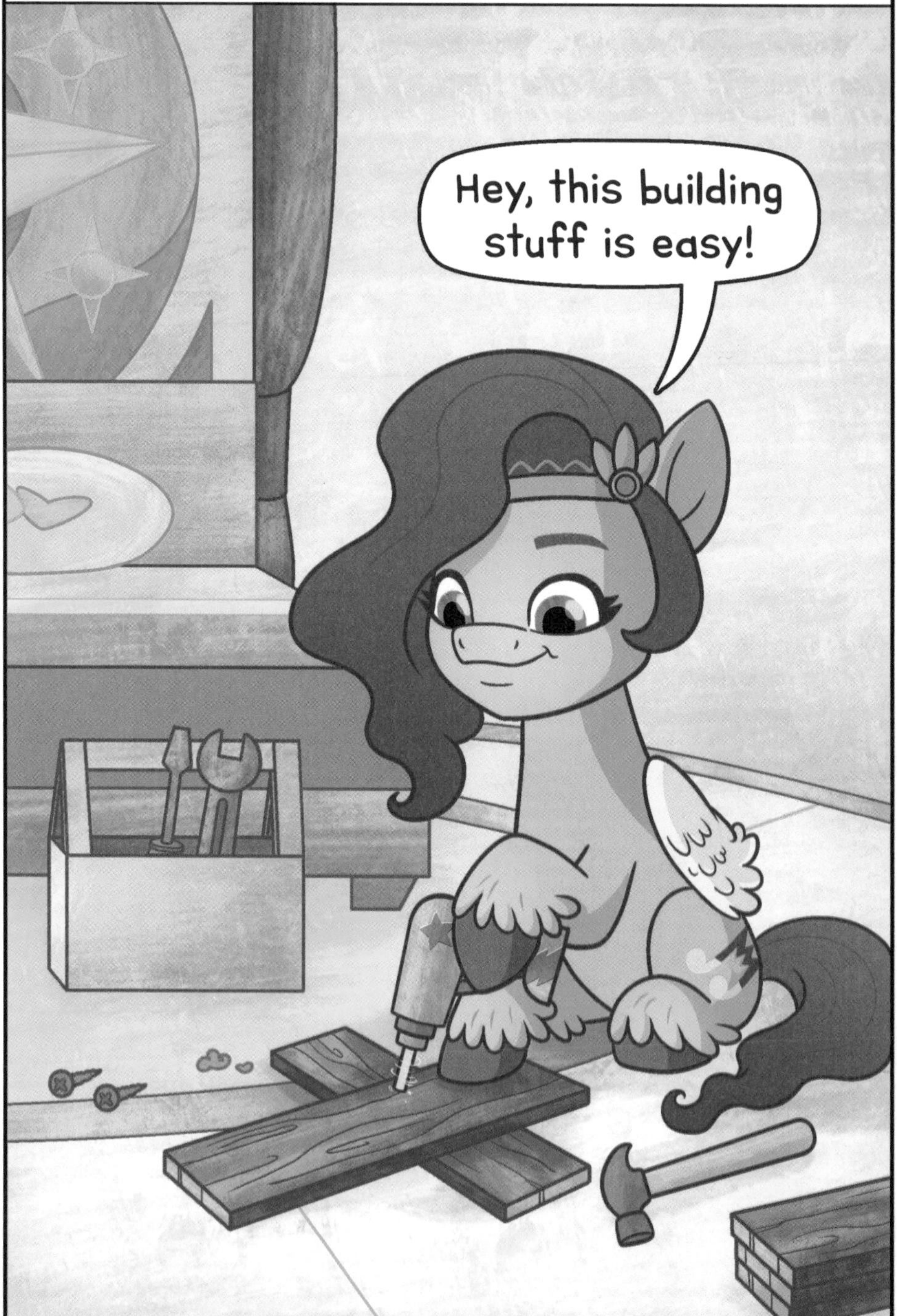
Hey, this building stuff is easy!

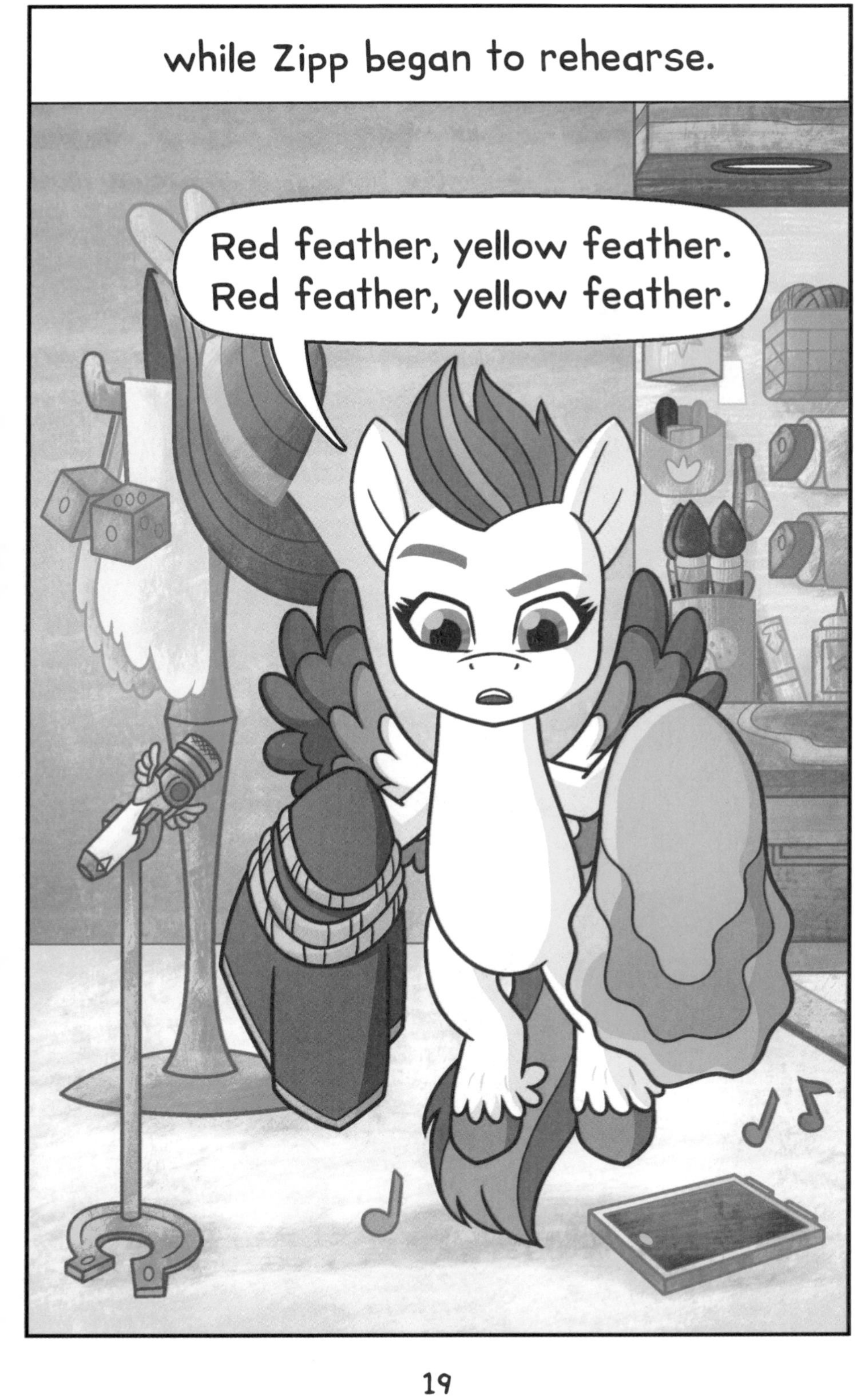
while Zipp began to rehearse.
Red feather, yellow feather. Red feather, yellow feather.

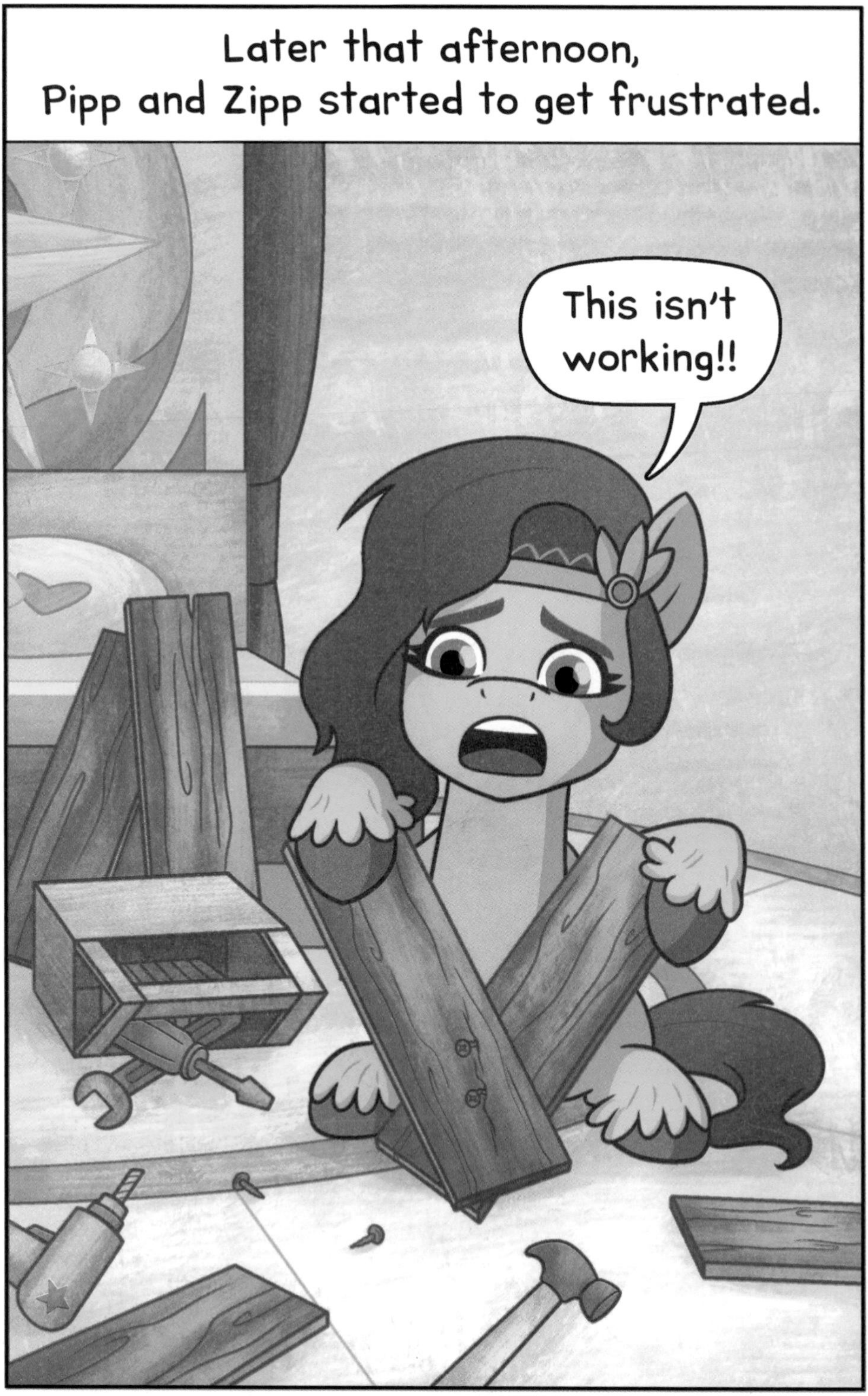
Later that afternoon,
Pipp and Zipp started to get frustrated.
This isn't working!!

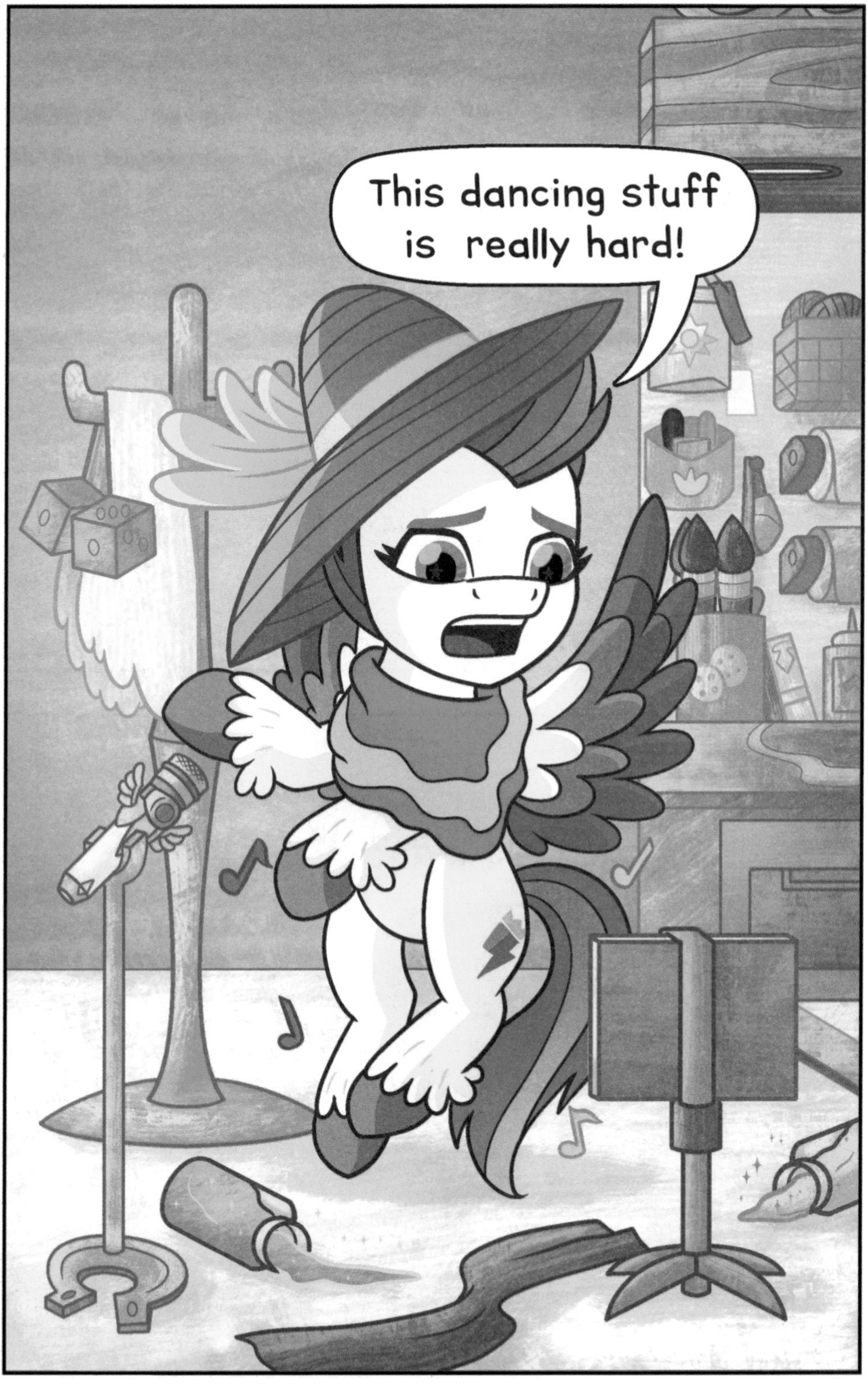
This dancing stuff is really hard!

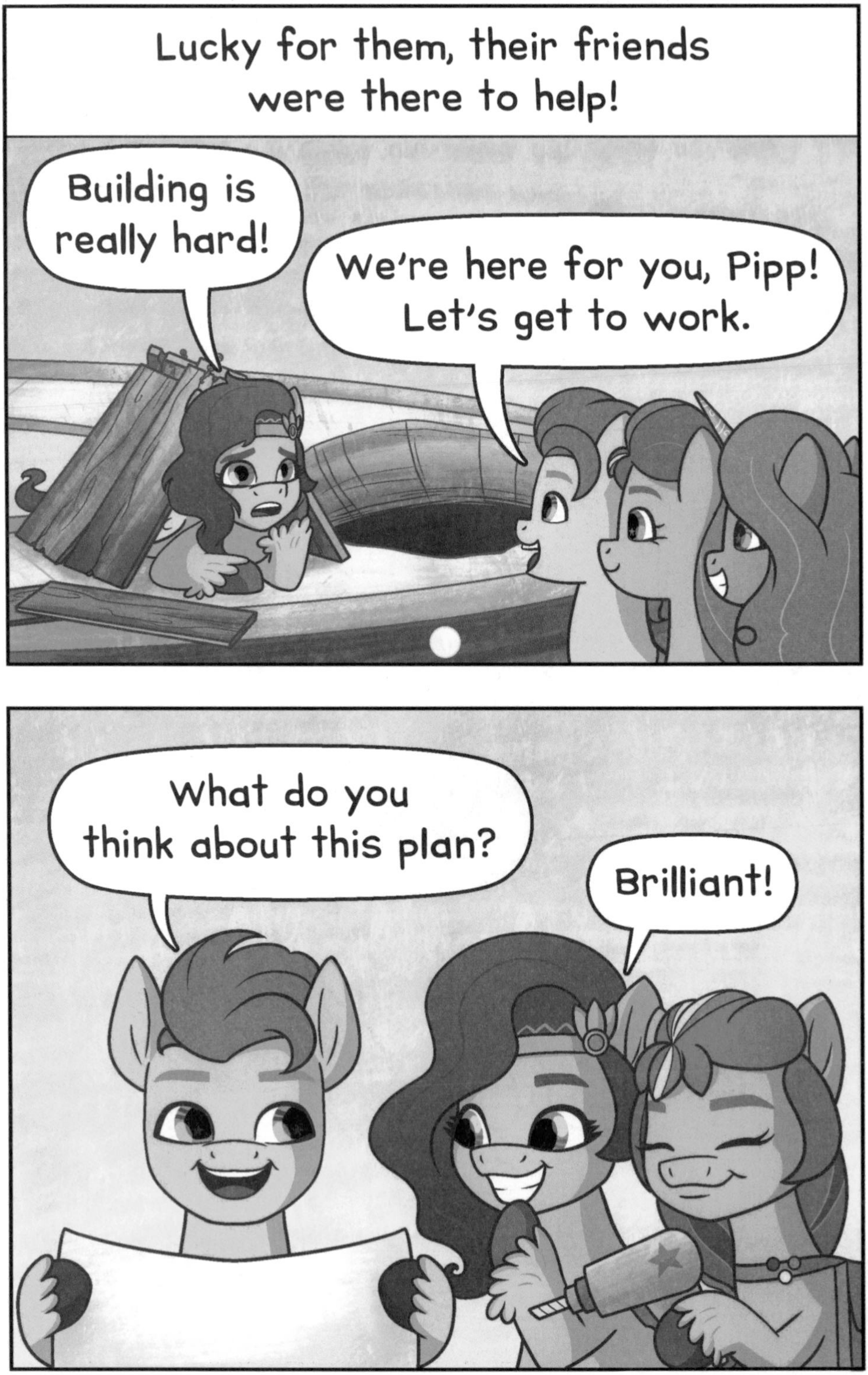
Lucky for them, their friends were there to help!
Building is really hard!
We're here for you, Pipp! Let's get to work.
What do you think about this plan?
Brilliant!

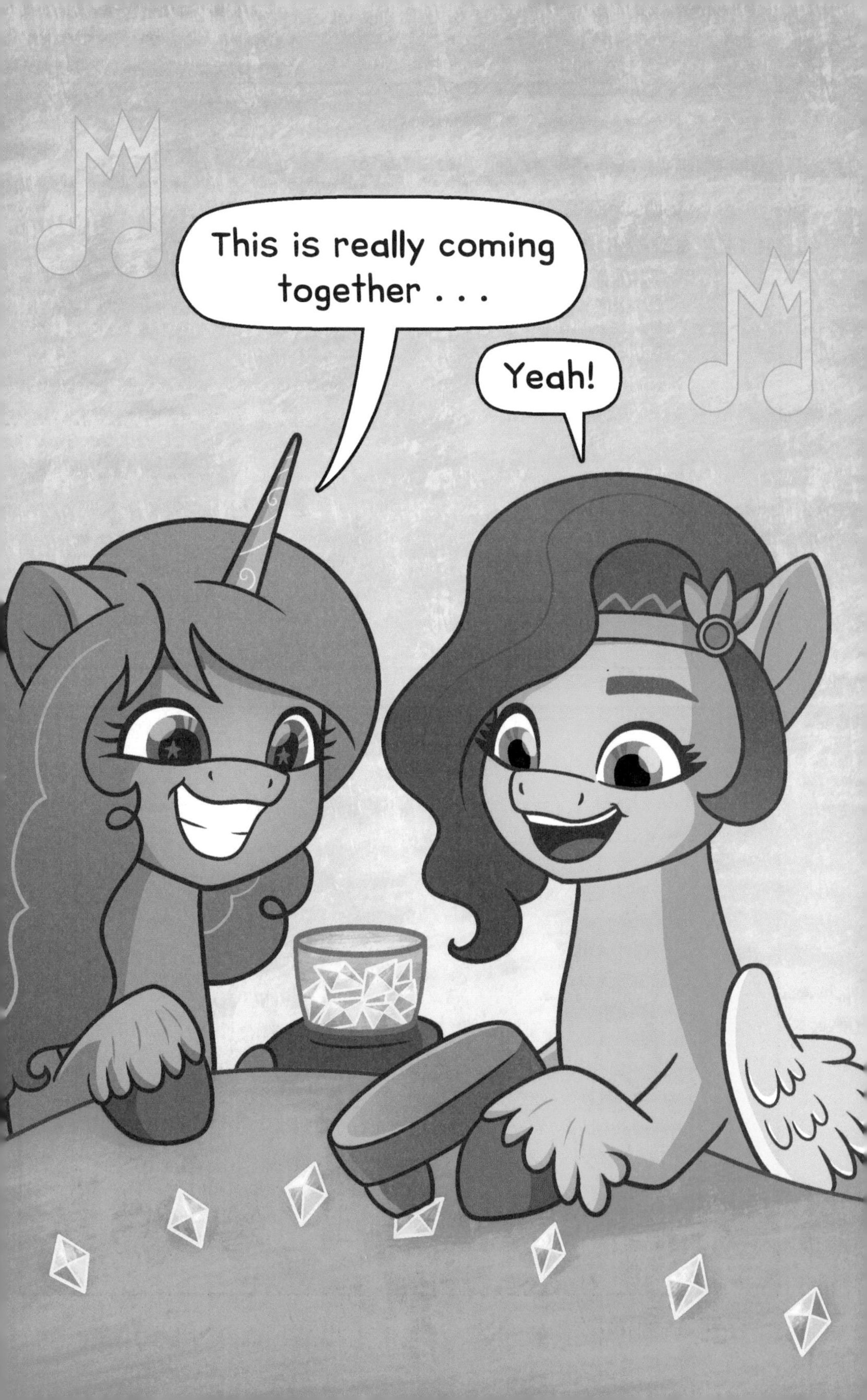
This is really coming together . . .
Yeah!

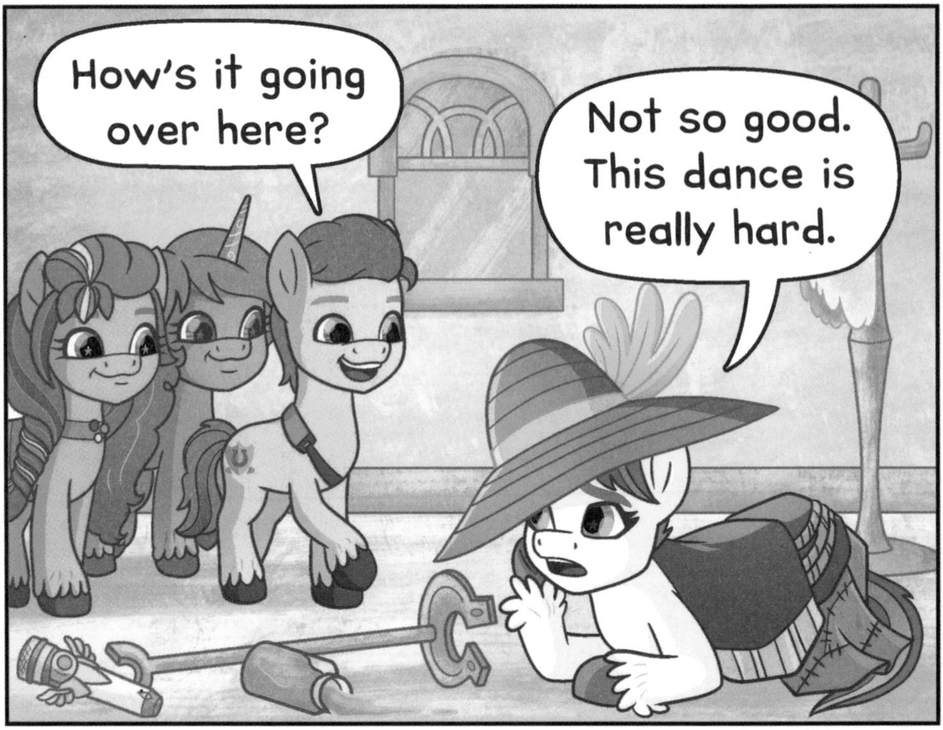
How's it going over here?
Not so good. This dance is really hard.

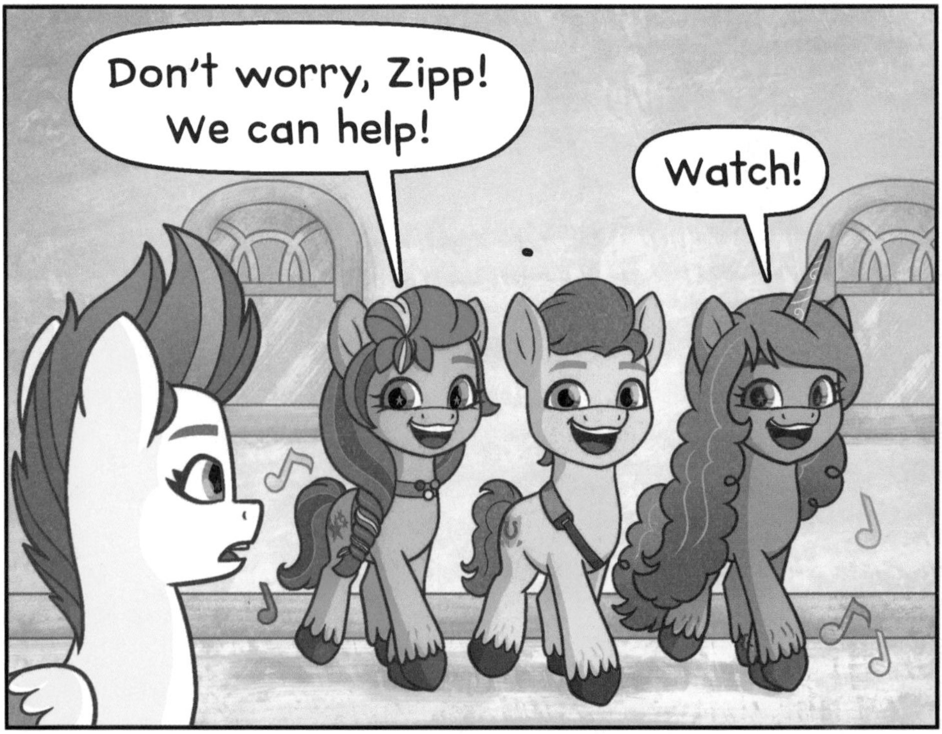
Don't worry, Zipp! We can help!
Watch!

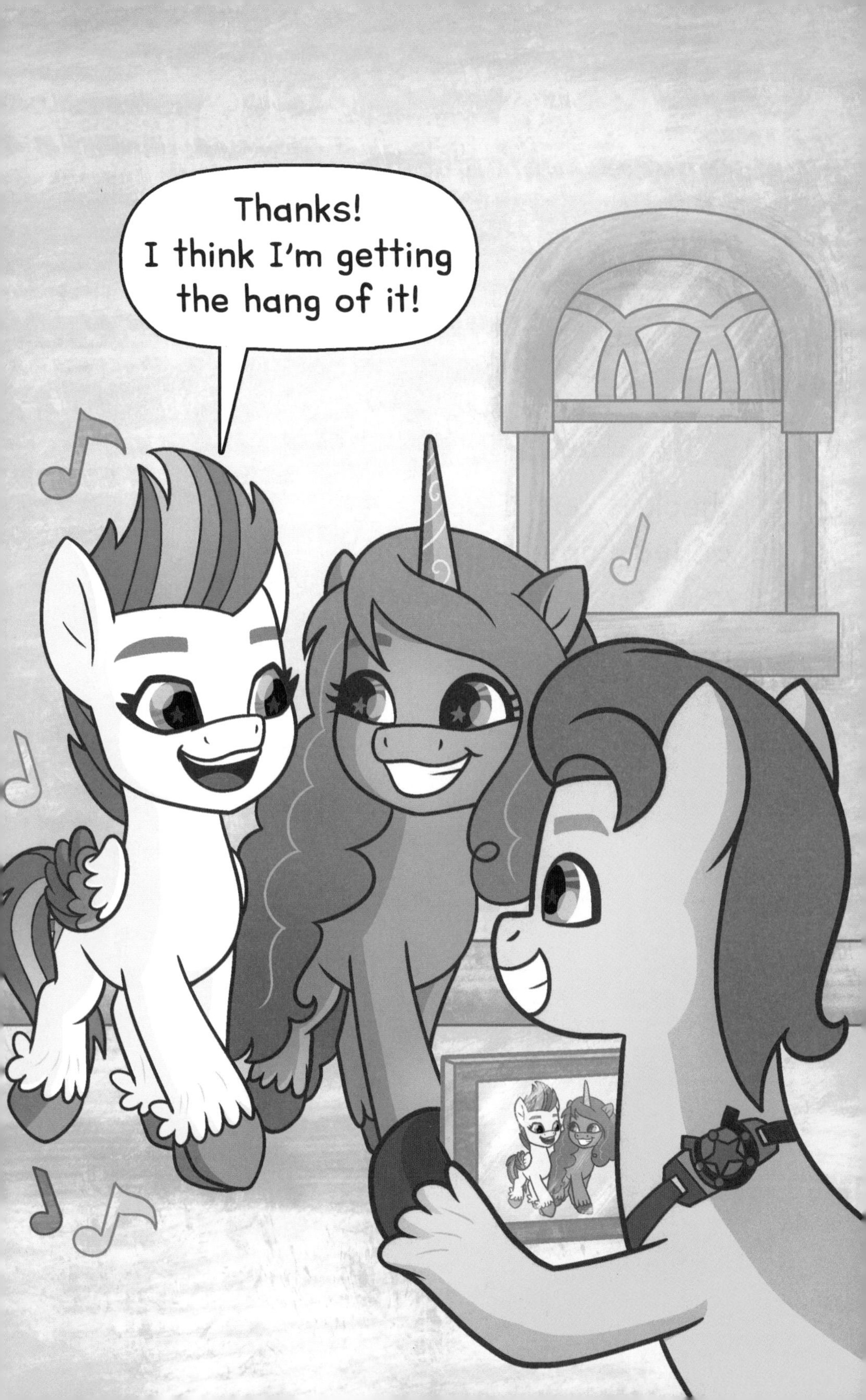
Thanks! I think I'm getting the hang of it!

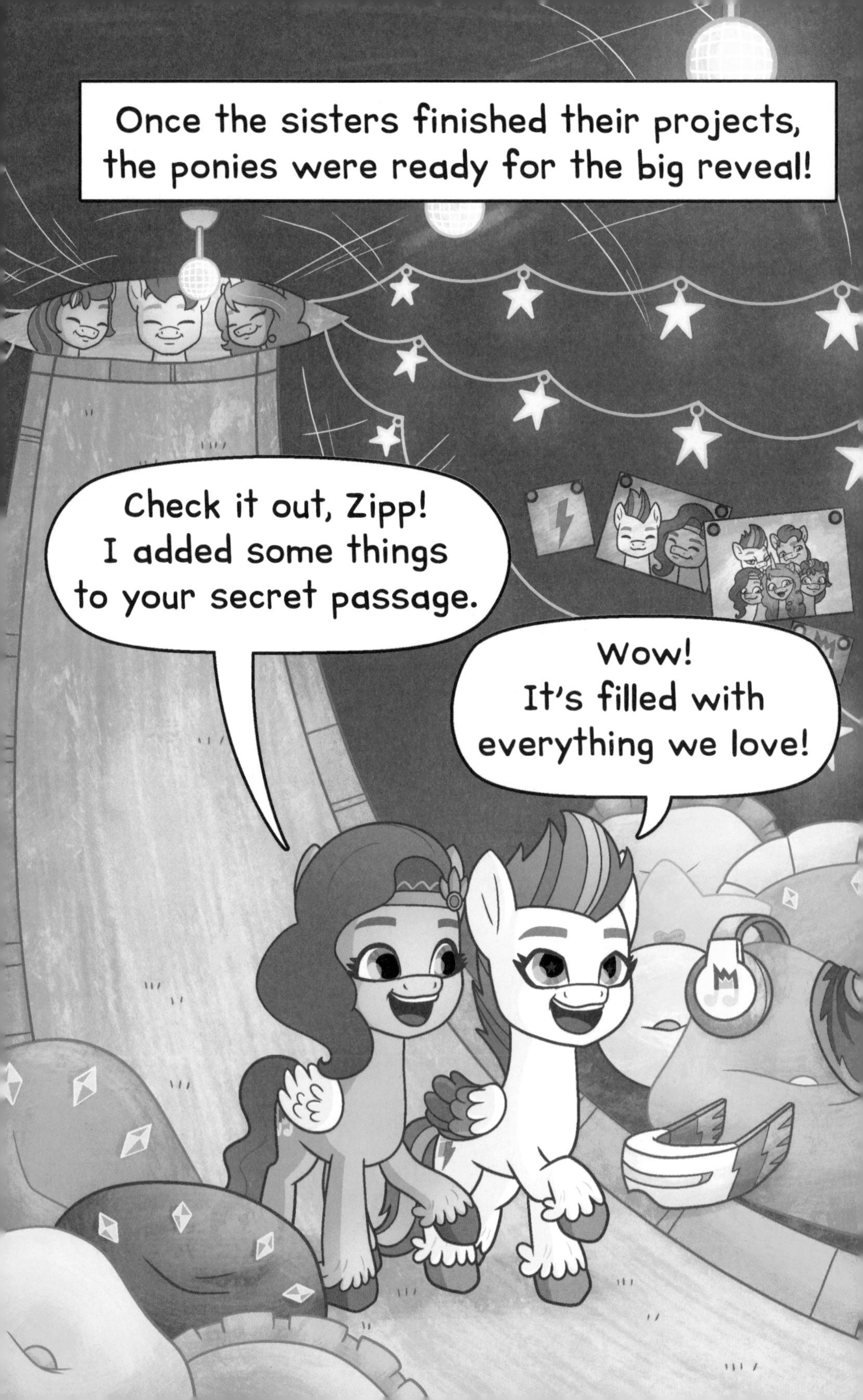
Once the sisters finished their projects, the ponies were ready for the big reveal!
Check it out, Zipp! I added some things to your secret passage.
Wow! It's filled with everything we love!

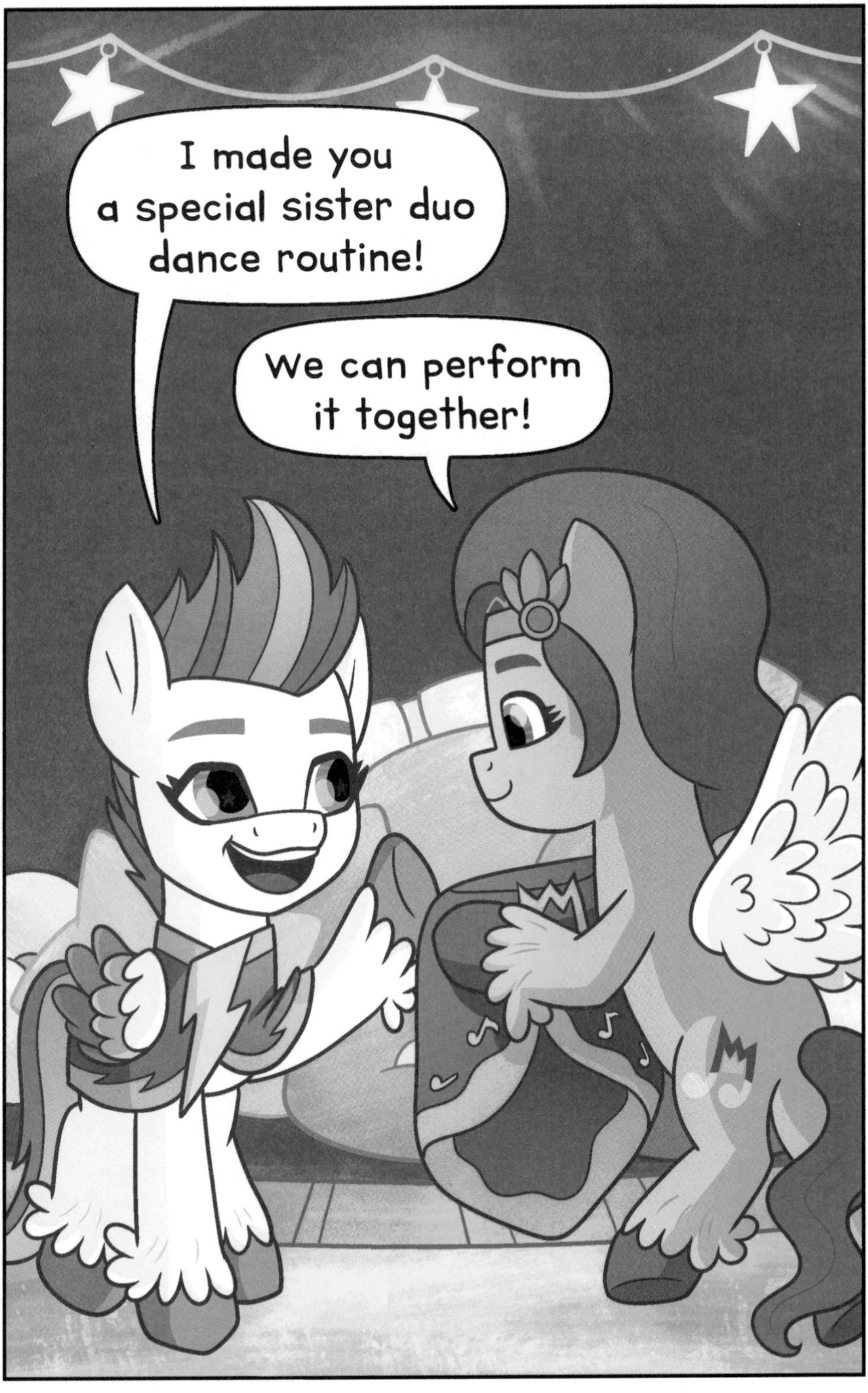
I made you a special sister duo dance routine!
We can perform it together!

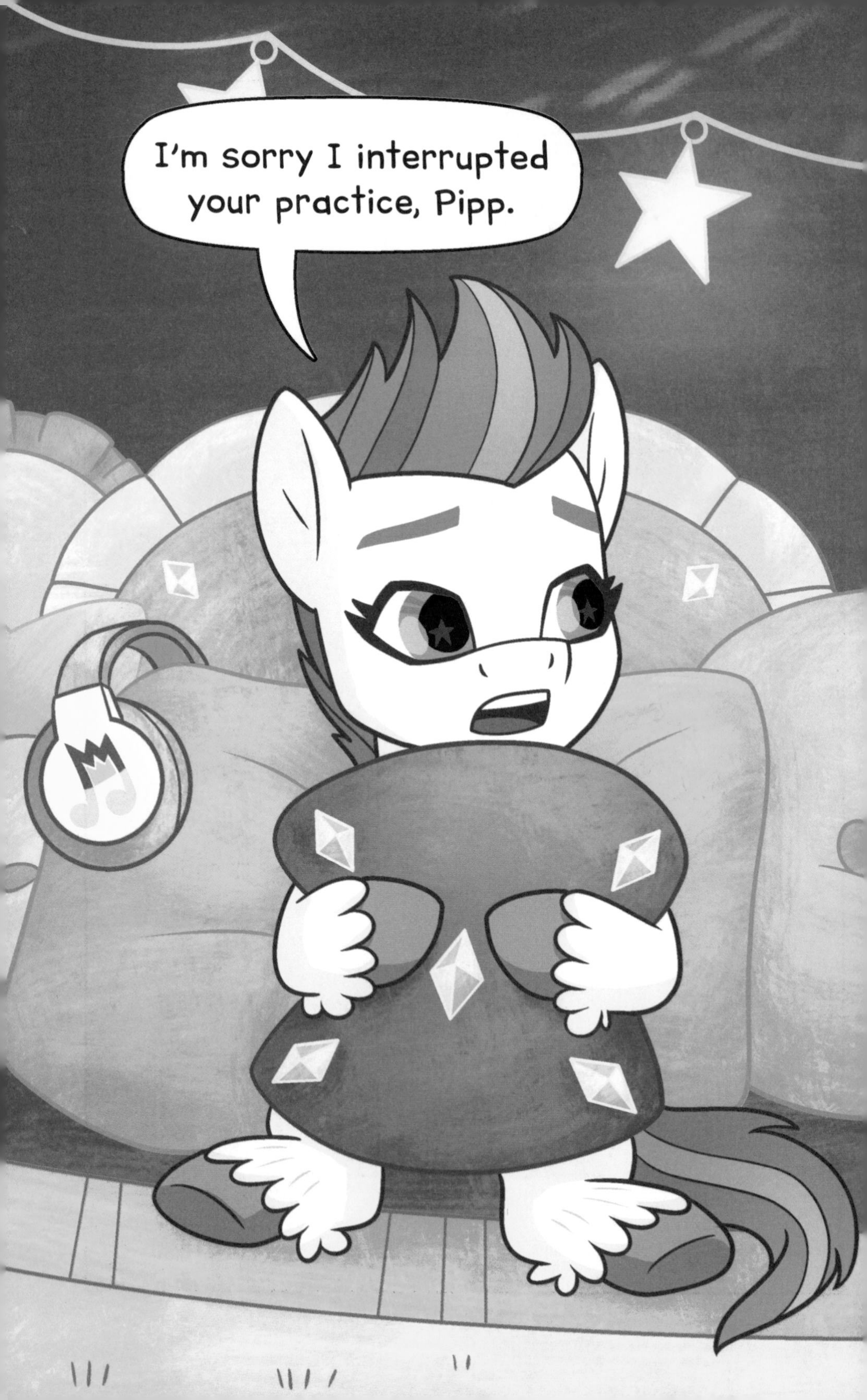
I'm sorry I interrupted your practice, Pipp.

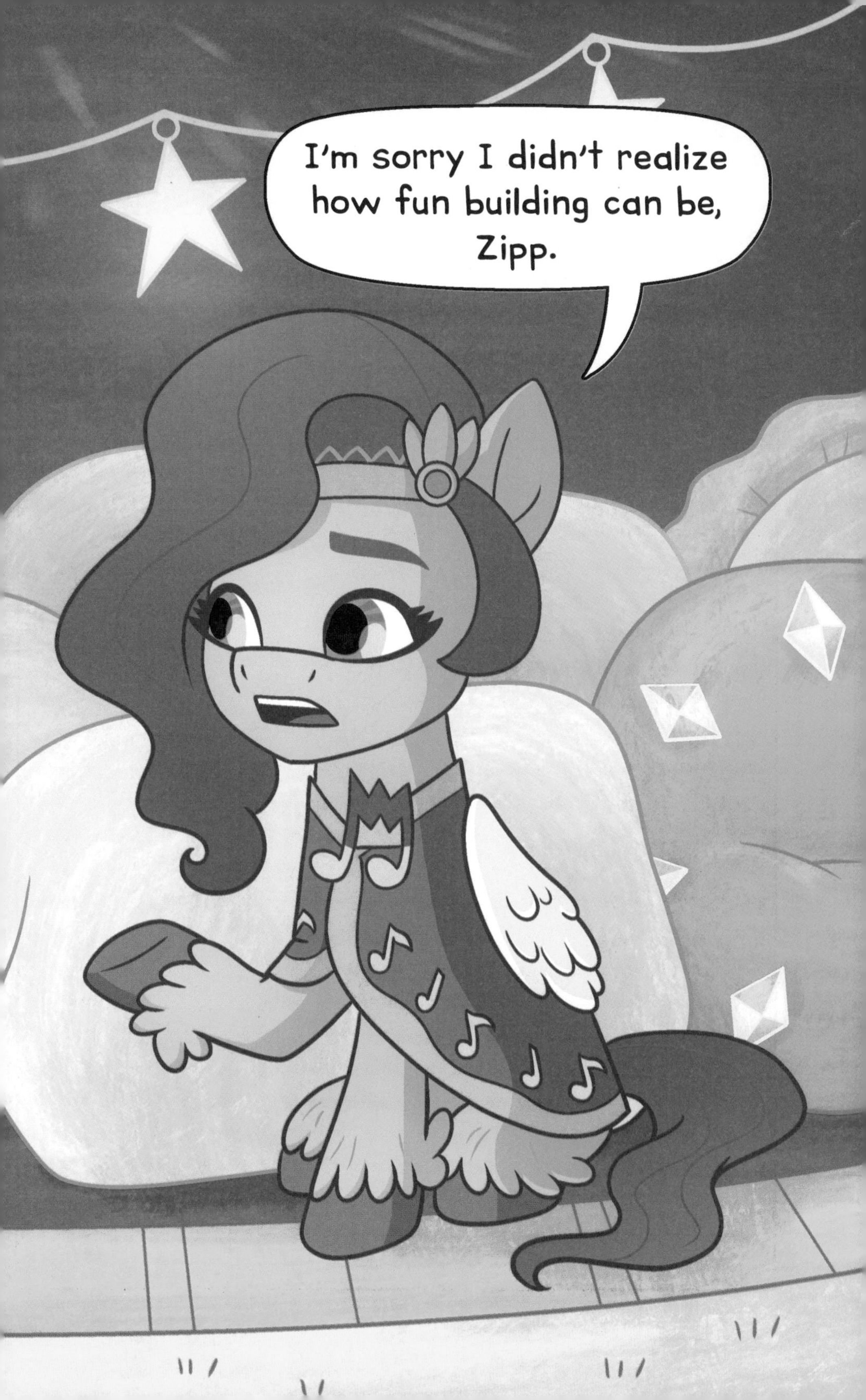
I'm sorry I didn't realize how fun building can be, Zipp.

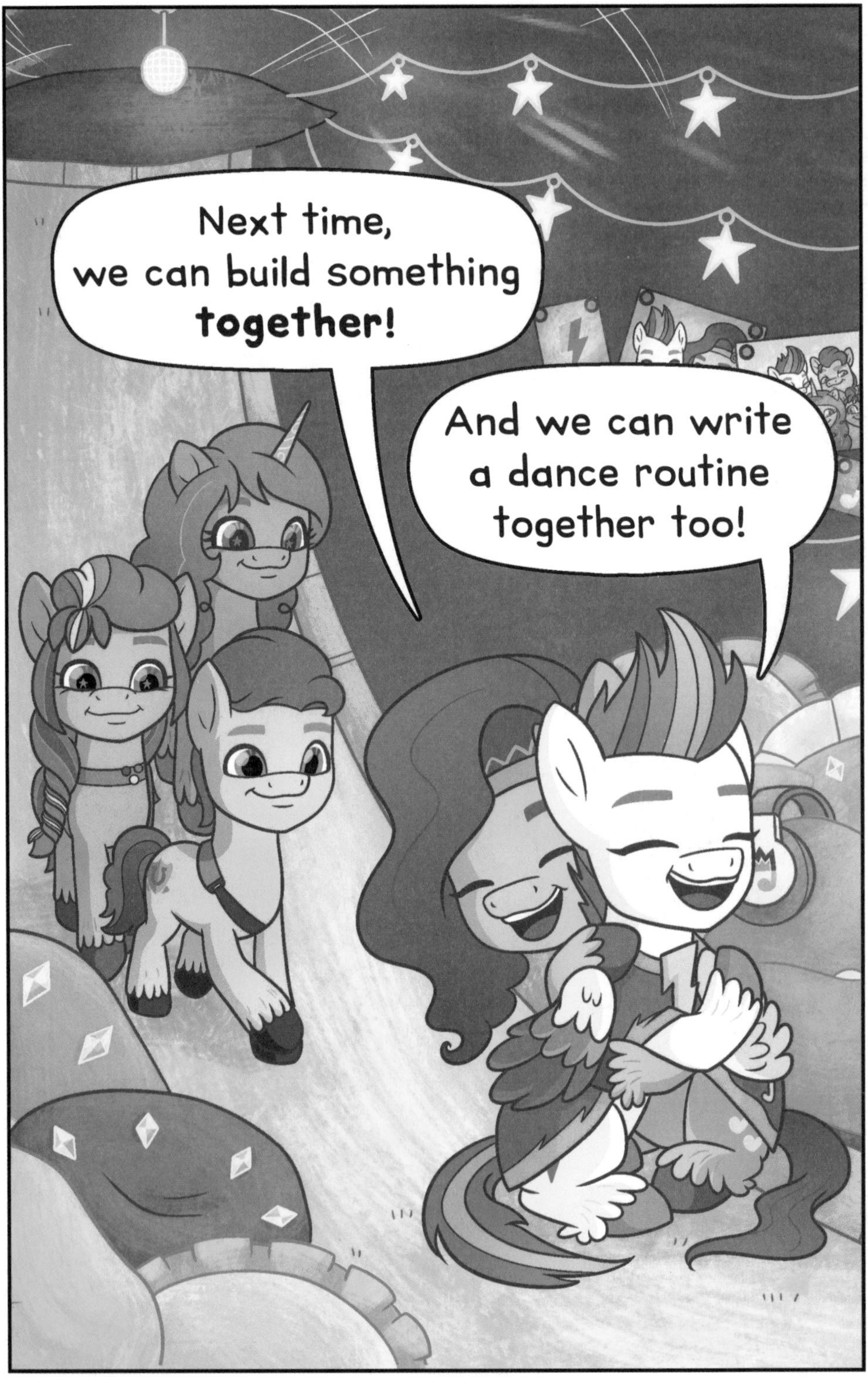
Next time, we can build something **together!**
And we can write a dance routine together too!

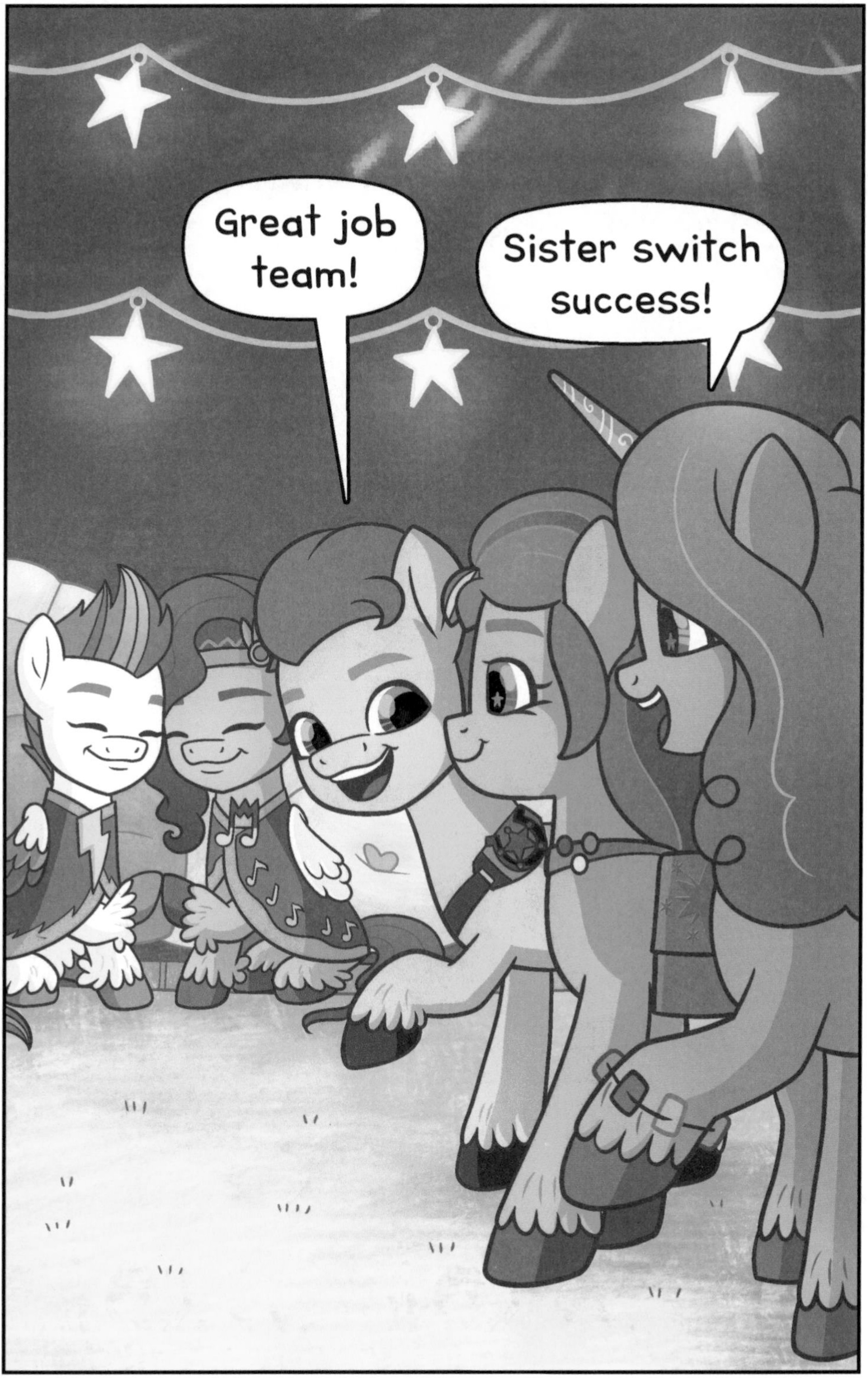
Great job team!
Sister switch success!

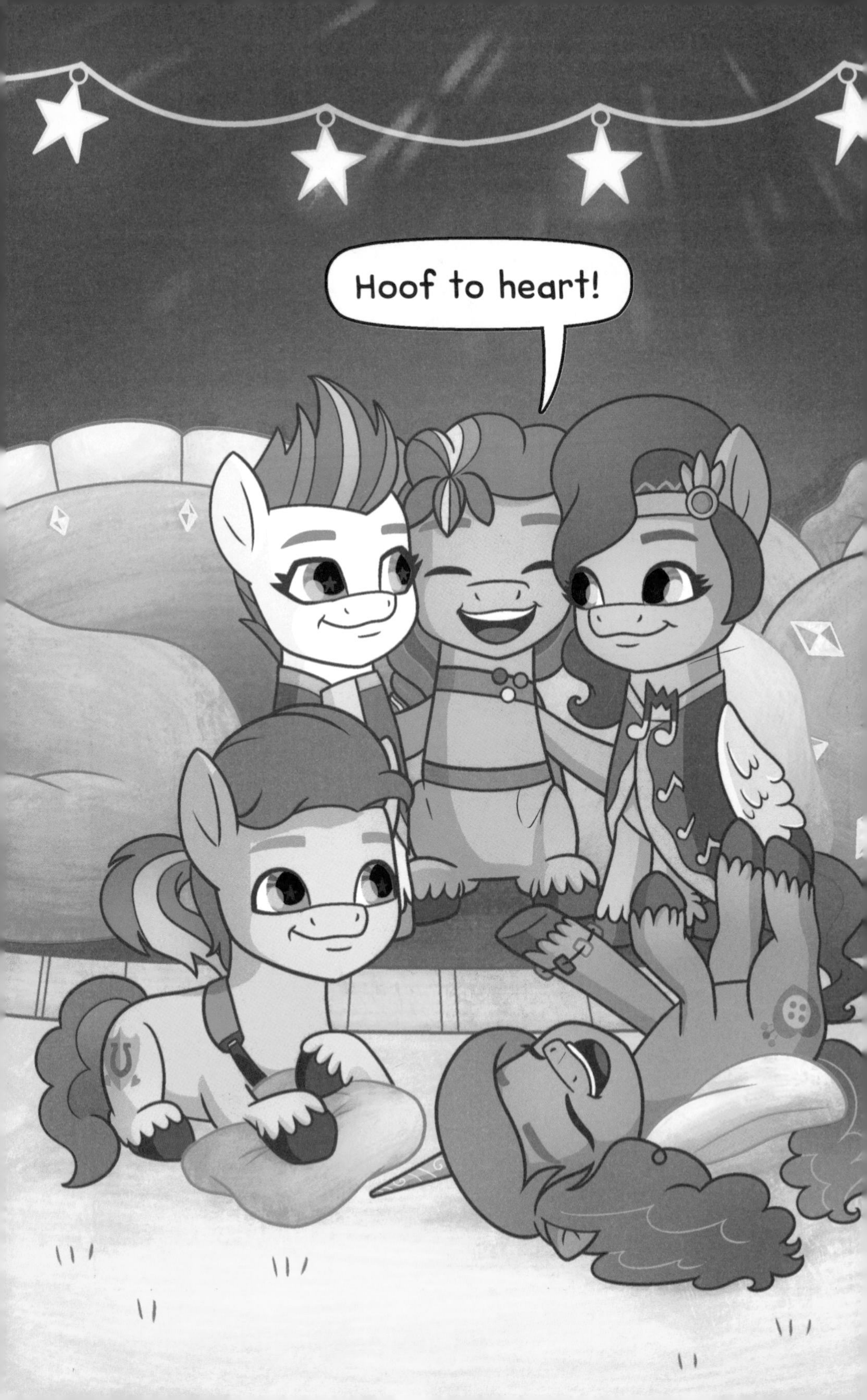
Hoof to heart!